B

10

I've travelled the world twice over,
Met the famous: saints and sinners,
Poets and artists, kings and queens,
Old stars and hopeful beginners,
I've been where no-one's been before,
Learned secrets from writers and cooks
All with one library ticket
To the wonderful world of books.

SPARROW'S YARD

The love story of Iris and Johnny began in Sparrow's Yard, an old established market. Johnny's father, Cyril Redmayne, owned it and Iris's mother, Melia Crockett, was a stall-holder. Cyril Redmayne's hatred of the stall-holders dated from his boyhood when they were the innocent cause of a rift between his parents, leading to his subsequent unhappiness. Melia foresaw that a romance between her daughter and his son would cause problems but she was not prepared for the action Redmayne took to break up their children's romance.

Books by Audrey Curling
in the Ulverscroft Large Print Series:

THE RUNNING TIDE
SPARROW'S YARD

AUDREY CURLING

SPARROW'S YARD

Complete and Unabridged

ULVERSCROFT
Leicester

First published in Great Britain in 1964 by
Hurst & Blackett Ltd.,
London

First Large Print Edition
published September 1987

British Library CIP Data

Curling, Audrey
Sparrow's Yard.—Large print ed.—
Ulverscroft large print series: romance
I. Title
823′.914[F]   PR6053.U7

ISBN 0-7089-1683-X

Published by
F. A. Thorpe (Publishing) Ltd.
Anstey, Leicestershire
Set by Rowland Phototypesetting Ltd.
Bury St. Edmunds, Suffolk
Printed and bound in Great Britain by
T. J. Press (Padstow) Ltd., Padstow, Cornwall

1

SOMEONE was playing a saxophone. The tune was haunting and sweet and it penetrated the classrooms of the Practical Wing at Abbeyfield Technical College, where there was so much feverish activity going on that no one except a girl called Iris Crockett seemed to notice it.

Iris was one of Mrs. Drew's dress students, all of whom were getting ready for the fashion parade they were to stage that afternoon before they broke up for Christmas.

It was always hard to keep the atmosphere calm on these occasions and Mrs. Drew noticed Iris Crockett particularly at that moment. She was standing by her ironing board absolutely motionless with a look on her face like that of a child waking from a nightmare.

Mrs. Drew was sure there was something wrong because Iris had cut a class again that week, so she beckoned her into the adjoining stock room where it was quiet. She did not expect it to be easy to find out what the trouble was, for the girl had always been reticent, so she tried to put her at her ease by praising her work and saying she was sure her mother would be pleased when she saw her in the parade.

"My mother can't come," Iris said awkwardly. "She's very sorry but she has to go somewhere else."

"If only she would enlarge a little and say where," Mrs. Drew thought, but she scarcely ever mentioned her family and her mother had never yet attended a college function.

"Is anything worrying you?" she asked kindly.

Iris shook her head and Mrs. Drew said: "I wish you'd tell me if there is. I might be able to help, you know."

She waited, but when Iris was still silent she took the direct approach.

"Why did you miss science yesterday?" she asked.

"I—I had a headache," stammered Iris.

"Then you should have been in the rest room and you weren't. You were not in the college at all, were you? This is the third time you've missed that class and I must know why. You can't have a head-ache every Thursday afternoon."

Iris was clutching one hand in the other; her eyes were very bright and her cheeks were flushed. "You won't let my mother know, will you?" she said in a strained voice.

"That depends. Look, Iris, I want to help you. Don't you trust me?"

"Yes, but you'd never understand. I should never have come to Abbeyfield," Iris blurted out. "I should have stayed home to help Ma. It's so hard for her with no one but Uncle Wally and when they start to build offices just where we keep our stall we don't know what will happen."

Mrs. Drew had had no idea until that moment that the Crocketts' greengrocery business was only a market stall and she began to understand a great many things about Iris that had puzzled her.

"I can see why you've looked so worried lately," she sympathized. "Does this mean you have to find another pitch?"

"We hope we can stay but everyone says our square's bound to be turned into a car park for the offices, and it's not only that,

Mrs. Drew. We depend on Uncle Wally's horse and cart for transport and that can't go on for ever, so I'm learning to drive a van."

"Does it all fall on you, then?" Mrs. Drew asked gently.

"There's no one else," Iris said. Then she added in a low voice: "It would be so different if Tom were home."

"Tom?" queried Mrs. Drew.

"My brother. Ma's gone to see him today. We must keep the stall going for Tom, so that's all the more reason why I should help."

"Does he have to be away?" asked Mrs. Drew.

Iris looked suddenly appalled. Her hand flew to her mouth in dismay. She had said too much and as though to mock her the saxophone began to play that tune again— the one that always took her back to the last evening when Tom was home. As though she were bewitched by the music she began to tell Mrs. Drew all about it. Breaking through her usual wary reserve she told her things she had never told anyone else and once she began she could not stop.

She told her how hopeful they had all felt at home when Tom returned after a year in prison and how certain her mother had been that he would never go back. He had promised to pull the business up and make it as prosperous as it had been in his father's day.

As she told Mrs. Drew all this Iris felt an immense relief because the teacher's understanding was something she had never expected. She even told her about that last evening when Tom took them to a dance—herself and Ma.

"She was so happy! Everything was marvellous—Tom home, and me getting a place here. Things couldn't have been better. Then the music stopped. One minute we were dancing and the next he was being taken away. He'd been in a wage hold-up. Our Tom! Oh, Mrs. Drew, I shan't ever forget how he looked when they took him away—like a frightened little boy. And Ma . . ."

She could not go on, but Ma's image burned behind her eyes. Ma in the tight-fitting, shiny dress she had bought to celebrate Tom's return to respectability. It was a bold, luscious red embroidered with sequins and its incongruity seemed to emphasize the horror of the evening. On the way home afterwards in the bus, surrounded by people to whom nothing unusual had happened, she and Ma had shared a dazed feeling of disbelief and in the days that followed they found crazy hopes to cling to right up to the moment when the four-year sentence annihilated them.

"And he's only served two," she said. "It seems like a lifetime already."

Mrs. Drew had never expected a revelation like this. She would never have guessed, looking at Iris, that she lived against this disturbed and sometimes violent background.

"When I pass my driving test we could have a van and then think how I could help. We might even start a vegetable round! That's why I cut science yesterday —for a driving lesson."

"But what about your work here?" asked Mrs. Drew. "It's terribly important for you to pass your examination. You can be a great help at home when you get a good job."

"I know, but once I have this test off

my mind I'll be able to concentrate ever so much better, Mrs. Drew. Really I will."

A note of optimism had given a lift to the girl's voice and her face was eager. She was appealing for encouragement and she needed it. A market stall, antiquated transport and a brother in prison! Mrs. Drew had not the heart to quench her.

"Things may turn out a lot better than you expect," she said. "Tom may even be home before they start on those offices."

"It's just that sometimes it all seems to swamp me," Iris said.

"I can understand that but don't let it rob you of your chances," Mrs. Drew said. "I shall see you get some extra coaching for those lessons you missed. Now don't look so anxious! I shan't tell anyone what you've confided in me."

Iris gave a sigh of relief. "No one here has a clue but it takes me all my time to remember," she said. "I once told Caroline Golding that Tom was an officer in the Navy and she'll never forget it."

While they had been talking the hubbub from the classroom had swelled in volume and they returned to find that it had been invaded by six of the hairdressing students, five of whom were dressing out their models' hair, while the sixth, Caroline Golding, sat on a table swinging her legs and munching an apple.

"Just look at that clock!" Mrs. Drew exclaimed. It was time for lunch, but as she gathered up her register and papers a clamour of voices broke out begging for help and advice.

"Now keep calm all of you," she implored. "Relax, have your lunch, and I shall be back as soon as I've had mine."

As the door closed behind her Caroline said: "Come on, Iris. Let's get a move on with that wig of yours."

Iris was still thinking of her conversation with Mrs. Drew and she looked at Caroline blankly. "Sorry," she said. "I was thinking of something else."

"I should just say you were. What's he like? I bet he's a beat and smokes hemp," said Caroline.

"Then you'd lose. He's six foot tall, he's twenty-six and his hair waves."

"You should forget him. He's spoiling your expression. Aren't you going to eat anything?"

8

"I'm not hungry and I forgot my sandwiches anyway," Iris said.

"Share mine," Caroline offered, producing a packet from her basket. "What are you doing for Christmas?"

"Staying at home," Iris said.

"So am I. Will your brother be on leave?"

"Not this Christmas," said Iris.

"Oh, what a shame. I was going to ask you to bring him over. Could you come yourself? We have crowds of people in every day and it's quite fun even though the oldies are there. How about it?"

"Well, I might be able to come on Tuesday," Iris said.

"Then that's a date. Don't forget. I say, does your brother want a pen friend? What's the name of his ship?"

"My brother hates writing letters, he loathes little girls and he's just changing ships," said Iris hurriedly. "Now I'm going to put my dress on before you start on my hair."

She went into a changing cubicle and shut the door, thankful to be away from Caroline's questions for a few minutes. She felt as though she had run a race and although the day was cold and the classroom not overheated she was sweating. She really had got to keep calm, for it would be the end if she were to spoil the new dress.

There was a tap at the door. "Do you want any help?" Caroline asked, poking her head in.

Her face was piquantly pretty. She had high cheek bones and light brown eyes which were inclined to slant up at the corners. Her mouth was rather large and her lips well shaped and she had perfect teeth. It was a delight to see her because she always looked so happy.

Suddenly Iris thought: "How I wish I had her luck. A mother and a father and no one inside! I wonder what it feels like?"

"My, that dress!" Caroline exclaimed, "It's *dramatic*! Here, let me hold it for you. . . ."

Iris slid into the dress and stood before the glass smoothing it down over her hips. It was a plain, heavy silk sheath of a brilliant, emphatic colour like an African violet.

"We dyed the material ourselves," she said. "Success, would you say? I knew the exact shade I wanted—something sudden like a splash of ink on a page. What do you think? Does it do anything for me?"

"Everything!" declared Caroline enthusiastically. "With your fair hair it's just fab."

"We'd better go outside," Iris said, "the cubicles will be wanted."

The classroom was like a cage of birds. A record player kept up an incessant din and several of the students were doing the twist, their faces serious, their mouths crammed with food.

Iris put her overall on and sat before a mirror and Caroline drew a brush firmly through her hair.

"I've got to help Mrs. Drew receive the guests, so don't get too wild with that brush," Iris said.

"You'll look super super stunning when I've done with you," Caroline assured her.

"I shall simply love myself if I do. There's a simply gorgeous dark blue skirt and jacket to go over this sheath—the colours are sheer bliss together. You'll see what I mean when I come down the cat walk."

"Gracious, you're a genius. Did it cost a terrible lot?"

"Two ten," Iris said laconically. "Remnants."

Caroline sighed. "If my mother hears that she'll create because I took up hair-dressing," she remarked.

Iris had natural ash-blonde hair which she usually wore in a page-boy bob, but having already seen a sketch of her dress Caroline was swathing it into a shining cone.

"There!" she said at last, holding up a mirror so that the full effect of her work could be seen. "I'd say you look twenty years old and glamorous. What do you think?"

"Um—it's ever so dignified," said Iris. "I feel really mature."

She stood up and took her overall off.

"My!" exclaimed Caroline. "I don't know if it's the dress or the hair but you look—well—you look like someone apart —someone quite different from the rest of us."

Iris stared, her mouth open, the excited flush draining from her face.

"Oh no!" she cried. "Please, no! I don't

want to look different. Now I shall be scared of parading down that cat walk with everyone watching."

"Nobody who looks like you needs to be afraid of anything," Caroline said. "Here, have a drop of coffee out of my flask."

Iris was grateful for the coffee. It would not be long before the reception began now and although she would have liked her mother to be there she knew Aunt Camille would appreciate the fashion parade more. Aunt Camille! The mere thought of her brought a feeling of safety and comfort. She finished the coffee and put on her overall again.

"I'm going to the front door to look out for Aunt Camille," she told Caroline, pronouncing the name with what she hoped was the correct accent. At home they all pronounced it like the species with the hump—"Camel".

It was a relief to get away from the atmosphere of the classroom and to feel the cold, crisp air that flooded the entrance hall whenever anyone opened the outer doors. It was heaven to be alone. Out here, away from the others, she was sure of her identity. She was Iris Crockett of Lantern

13

Place and Sparrow's Yard and there was no pretence about her. In class she always had to keep her wits about her in case she gave the family secrets away. She had been caught off her guard when she told Mrs. Drew so much, but she did not regret it, for there had been none of the shocked surprise she dreaded.

At that moment her aunt entered the hall and stood with one hand resting on the long umbrella she carried, leaning forward a little almost as though she were waiting for an invisible curtain to go up. She wore a theatrical-looking cloak and a large hat that made her conspicuous in spite of her slight figure.

"Oh, Auntie, I never thought you'd get here so soon," said Iris, running over to her. "I *am* glad to see you!"

"Early doors. I can't help it, dear," her aunt replied. "My word, that hair style alters you."

"Do you like it?" Iris asked.

"It's beautiful. You look composed and superior," Aunt Camille replied, slipping her hand into Iris's and giving it an encouraging little squeeze. "But I like it the other way best," she added.

14

"It's only for today," Iris said. "I shall be myself again tomorrow."

"You look pale, ducky. Like a bit of chocolate?" Aunt Camille asked.

Iris took the proffered piece. "I ought to be back in class," she said, but she hesitated, wondering whether or not to put the question that was tormenting her. Then she decided and said quickly:

"Did you see Ma off? Was she all right?"

"Quite all right, dear," Aunt Camille replied. "You'd never have thought but that she was going to see someone in hospital. Try not to notice if she's quiet when we get home. It would upset her much more if she couldn't go to see Tom."

"It's so horrid at Christmas," Iris said, "and for days after she's thinking all the time." She paused, and then broke out with "Sometimes I think he'll never be good!"

"Come now, it's no use going on like that. You must hope, and you must believe, too," Aunt Camille said firmly. "You won't help if you let this get the better of you, Iris."

"I expect you're right," Iris admitted

after a moment. "But oh, how I wish we didn't live on the brink of a precipice all the time!"

The trickle of visitors into the hall was increasing to a stream so that it was no longer possible to talk confidentially. In spite of her anxieties Iris was beginning to feel excited about the parade and the reception, for there was always something thrilling about the functions at Abbeyfield.

"Gosh, isn't it wonderful to think I'm here, Auntie!" she said impulsively.

"Wonderful. A dream come true," Aunt Camille agreed. "Oh, I nearly forgot— Gran sent her love and so did Uncle Wally."

As Iris turned to go Aunt Camille caught her hand and whispered: "Good luck, ducky. Don't forget, whatever happens we shall all stick together the same as we've always done, so you haven't a worry in the world!"

Iris returned the pressure of her aunt's fingers. Her confidence was returning. She knew the afternoon would be a success and, after all, the uncertainty over Sparrow's Yard had been there so long it was best forgotten. There was no sense in for ever cringing from a blow that might never fall.

2

THE train was packed on the way home and Aunt Camille and Iris had to stand. There was not room to open a newspaper, but they both noticed one passenger in city clothes who was so engrossed in a score that they were curious to know what it was.

"Doesn't he look nice?" Aunt Camille whispered. "He reminds me of someone, but I can't think who for the moment. He's a music student, I should think."

"In that natty little bowler? More like the Stock Exchange, I should say," suggested Iris.

He was completely oblivious of their interest and only had eyes for his score, but Iris wished he would glance her way. She wondered who he was and where he worked and to take her mind off him she returned to the subject of the afternoon. Mr. Golding had come and Caroline's success had added to her own pleasure.

"Very nice," he had said, after a

prolonged and rather amused inspection of Iris's hair. "Very nice indeed, my dear."

Iris was not used to meeting men of his type. His skin was fine and smooth and rather fair, not like the skins of people who earn their livings in the open, and although his face had lines on it they were different from those which creased her Uncle Wally's countenance. Uncle Wally's lines crissed and crossed as though his skin had been scrunched up like a piece of paper before being smoothed out and fitted to his face. When she was much younger she had wondered if it might be possible to iron it and once she had asked if she might try.

"I won't let you feed no more sugar to Dook if that's the sort of lip you give me," had been Uncle Wally's discouraging reply.

To those who did not know him Uncle Wally was a rather forbidding old man with a complete lack of social grace. Dook was his horse and his best friend. Now Iris began to wonder what life was like in other families—families like Caroline Golding's, for instance.

The young man managed to turn

another page of his score and she thought: "He's the same kind as the Goldings, too. They get a special look—those people."

At times she felt an almost savage pride in her own family and she loved each and every one of them from her grandmother, old Ascot Tagg to Uncle Harry, who was Aunt Camille's husband. And Tom. Perhaps especially Tom. It was strange and somehow frightening to be gripped by this knowledge that whatever happened, whatever they did or whatever they became, she would always have this deep, ineradicable feeling for them, this love.

"I think I'll go home by way of the Yard," she said as they neared their stop.

"I shall take the bus," Aunt Camille replied. "Oh, look, that nice young man is getting off here, too. And doesn't he move fast! He's gone already."

They were being borne along the platform on a tide of homebound Christmas shoppers, but now that the strange young man had streaked away Iris was not interested in any of them.

Suddenly Aunt Camille clutched her arm. "Look! There's Florrie Perks ahead," she warned. "Let's slow down a bit—we don't want to catch up with *her*."

Iris slackened her pace immediately. "Oh, gosh!" she groaned.

Florrie Perks wore a musquash coat, exaggeratedly high-heeled red shoes and gloves to match. She was hatless, and her rich, crisply curling auburn hair owed nothing to the hairdresser's art. Her face which was too heavily made up, must once have been beautiful; now it was prematurely haggard, but it was distinguished by her unusual eyes with their glitteringly light irises. She was not carrying any parcels and she descended the stairs slowly.

"My word, isn't she getting thin!" Aunt Camille exclaimed. "Dieting, I suppose. Spoilt herself. She was much prettier fat."

"Horrible thing," said Iris, for Florrie Perks was the woman who had stolen her father away and kept him long enough to bear him two children before he remembered his duty and came home to Ma.

Florrie was one of a large family of barrow folk, all of whom were truculent, pugnacious and knavish, and whenever there was a fight in a local pub a Perks

21

was sure to be at the bottom of it. Almost every barrow or stall pitched in Villa Park belonged to Florrie's brothers, uncles or cousins, and she owned a cottage at the end of the High Road with a dirty old shed where her mother had once skinned rabbits. Now she kept a coffee stall there and it was the last of its kind in the neighbourhood. She had plenty of customers, too, in spite of her unpredictable moods.

Iris always viewed Florrie Perks with curiosity and distrust, for she had been Ma's best friend, bridesmaid at her wedding to Quick Crockett, and then she had stolen him away, leaving poor Ma to bring up Tom alone.

Florrie's two children, Selina and Raymond, were a different matter and Iris accepted them because they were there before she was born. She never looked at them, as Ma would not have liked her to, but, after all, they were her own kith and kin, the children of her father, and there was no use denying it.

She was not altogether surprised to see Raymond now. He was at the bottom of the stairs and had obviously come to meet his mother. He was so like their father—

even more so than Tom was—that she never saw him without feeling her heart turn over. He had his mother's hair, but there was no mistaking Quick Crockett's eyes and features. Apart from his physical appearance Iris considered him a mess. He wore a black leather jacket, tight jeans and winkle-picker shoes, and he affected a swagger that did not come off. A ton-up boy who had never owned a bike—that was Raymond Perks.

He came forward to greet his mother as she reached the last step.

"How did you get on?" Iris heard him ask in an anxious tone.

"OK. You can stop worrying," Florrie answered. "Be going in after Christmas for a nice rest."

Aunt Camille and Iris took advantage of this encounter to hurry past but they were not quick enough to escape Florrie's sharp eyes.

"Why, Raymond, just look who's trying to push us over!" she bawled. Her voice was naturally loud and it possessed a penetrating quality which made it singularly compelling. "Dotty Camel Merritt and her stuck-up niece, upon my soul. Shove, why don't you?"

"Oh, shut up, Mum," begged Raymond. "You'll have everyone looking."

"And what a treat for 'em. They won't see a cloak and hat like that every day of the week," jeered Florrie. "Can't forget she was a conjuror's assistant, even though it was in the year dot. Bet she's got a nest of white mice in that hat!"

"Just ignore her," whispered Aunt Camille as she and Iris hurried to the exit. "People will think she's crazy."

"She must be," muttered Iris.

As they reached the street and joined the end of the bus queue they were thankful to see Florrie and her son cross the road without noticing them again.

"Dad must have been demented to leave Ma for that woman," Iris said bitterly. "I think so every time I see her."

"Well, dear, Quick always loved Ma but he just couldn't resist Florrie. Let's say he was bewitched for a time," said Aunt Camille. "Here's the bus."

Iris saw her aunt safely on board and then she stood and watched the bus go blustering away up the road. In spite of the Perkses she was glad to be home in Villa Park because she loved the place, and now she stepped out joyfully.

The High Road, towards which she was walking, had developed in a haphazard fashion and there were still a few huge Victorian houses which broke the continuity of the line of shops. One of the last of these had belonged to old Dr. Redmayne who had died the year before she went to Abbeyfield.

She remembered him gratefully, as did all her people, but he was an outcast in the eyes of his own family because he had allowed the forecourt of his house to degenerate into the place known as Sparrow's Yard, the little open-air market place where Amelia Arethusa Crockett, Uncle Wally Tagg, Winnie and Glad Cheek, the Tilley family and Princess Potter pitched their stalls and earned their living.

He had encouraged them there and they had prospered, trading with his blessing and with no need to hold licences or to conform to any rules but his. But now they existed uneasily from day to day, for Cyril

Redmayne, who had inherited his father's property, wanted to build an office block on the site of the old house. He was only waiting for official sanction to begin.

This did not necessarily mean that the stallholders would have to go and Mr. Redmayne had said they might stay, but that was on the day his father died and the fact that he had since refused the small rents they had always paid the old doctor made them suspicious. Then there were the rumours. When he builds his block the Yard will be wanted for a car park, people said. Stands to reason.

Iris always felt herself go quite cold at this, for she loved the Yard and could not imagine what life would be like without it. In the Yard she found colour and excitement. Fine springs and summers made it heaven; wind, rain, frost and cold could not rob it of its enchantment. She came to the Yard when she was happy and when she was sad and she always found something there to please or console her.

Now she was there, but something made her stop and catch her breath. There was a huge notice board in front of Dr. Redmayne's house. It was glaring white printed in red. The words on it seemed to jazz before her eyes, but each word gave her unspoken fears shape and reality.

She began to read from the beginning.

REDMAYNE HOUSE

High Road, Villa Park

OFFICE BLOCK

Builders: Jason, Brown & Sons
Architect & Engineers: Cyril Redmayne & Associates
Demolition: Parry, Marsh & Co.

The list of contractors continued and grew blurred as she looked and she put her hands behind her and felt the cold rough surface of the wall. It was rough to her touch and the ridges of cement between the bricks and the chill of it proved she was not dreaming.

She shut her eyes and tried to believe the board was not there and that nothing was going to change. But it was. They were going to pull down Dr. Redmayne's house and once it disappeared something no one could ever replace would go too.

The Yard was a square bounded on two sides by the blank side walls of shops and at the back by a hedge which grew some way in front of the house itself. A briar rose straggled over the hedge and in early summer its scent mingled with that of the lime trees in the garden.

Iris opened her eyes and the notice board was as threatening as before. It seemed to dominate the Yard and a partially erected hoarding hid most of the hedge. Uncle Wally was at their pitch opposite. He was covering up their stall with tarpaulins and she felt in a vague sort of way that he ought to look different. The Tilleys and the Cheeks had already gone, though it was before their usual time, but Princess Potter was still at her flower stall.

She had masses of chrysanthemums: gold, copper, crimson and white, and she had carnations and freesias, too. She was selecting some blooms for a customer, and her fingers, protruding from tatty, knitted mittens, were thick and purple with the cold. Her clothes were dark and shapeless but she had a bright, lively face. She caught sight of Iris as she gave her customer change and jerked her thumb in the direction of the notice board.

"Looks as though things are moving at last," she said. "Gave us all a nasty shock when they came and stuck that thing up today. Reckon I'd been kidding myself it would never happen."

"It won't do Ma much good," said Iris.

"No, duck. It's a bad job coming just before Christmas. Poor old Tilley's face was a sight to see, I can tell you. Still, I said to her, there's a long way to go before the building gets done."

"How long?" Iris asked.

"Going on two years, maybe. Never mind, Eh? Make the best of it. We're not dead yet."

Across the Yard Uncle Wally was sweeping up, meticulously chasing every vestige of waste up to the wall and then scraping it into a box between two pieces of board. When he finished there would not be so much as a sprout leaf or a tomato pip to show that vegetables had been sold there.

Iris was just about to cross over to him when a car nosed out through the opening in Dr. Redmayne's hedge. It came purring to a halt beside her and waited, its engine pulsing, till it could turn into the High Road. It was a Rolls, smooth, sleek and powerful. At the wheel was a middle-aged man with thin, greying hair and the same kind of skin that Mr. Golding had. There was a woman beside him in a mink coat who looked as though she had just come from a beauty parlour.

Suddenly the man turned his head and noticed Iris. He stared at her boldly and with admiration, but it was a cold look. His eyes were like blue glass. He looked her up and down, almost as though she were an object in a shop window and he were debating her worth. Then the woman beside him spoke and he turned to her. A second later there was a break in the flow of traffic and the Rolls glided into the High Road and sped off in the direction of the hill. The driver had not looked at Iris again, but she felt this omission was as deliberate as his scrutiny had been.

She hurried across the road.

"Does that board mean we shall be out of business, Uncle Wally?" she asked.

"Nah! 'Course it doesn't!" he answered

in an angry tone. "It'll bring us more trade. People passing in and out. They're bound to stop and buy—be the making of us."

"Yes, but suppose they make a car park —you know what people say."

"Take no notice of what people say," he said roughly. "Specially not when your Ma is by."

"Suppose they did, though? What would happen to Dook's stable?"

"No one's going to touch Dook's stable. They're going to build back by the hedge and that leaves us clear. You got other fish to fry, my girl, so just you fry 'em and don't think no more about that notice."

Iris knew that Uncle Wally's vehemence was only due to the insecurity which the notice board had brought so much nearer.

"All right, I'll try not to think," she said. But she only agreed to pacify him. "Are you going home now?" she asked.

He leant his broom against the wall and took a clay pipe out of his pocket, stuffed it with shag, lit it and took several puffs.

"You going to walk along of me all dolled up like that?" he grinned.

"Oh, come on. Let's get home," she said.

"Wait a minute, then. Got to put me broom away and see Dook all right."

He went into the stable and she heard him talking to Dook. She knew he hated to leave his horse and prolonged the parting as long as he possibly could. Often, in the night, he would creep out of the house he shared with his sister-in-law, old Ascot Tagg, and come down to the Yard just to make sure that Dook was safe from harm.

"Poor old Wally. That horse means a lot too much to him," Ascot would say. "Shame he didn't marry—it's gone to his head, you see."

"Oh, do come on, Uncle Wally," Iris called, for she knew the family would be waiting for them in Aunt Camille's front room at Lantern Place.

Another long minute went by before he joined her, then she tucked her hand through his arm and they set off down the High Road, Uncle Wally trotting briskly and Iris clicking along beside him on her high heels.

Presently she asked: "Who were the

32

people in the Rolls who came out of Dr. Redmayne's? There were a man and woman and he stared at me."

"You're asking for it—all dolled up like that."

"Well, who were they?" repeated Iris.

"Mr. and Mrs. Redmayne," he told her. "Used to know him once but he didn't ever know me."

"Why not?"

"Because he's a stuck-up, sour-eyed kipper," said Uncle Wally. "Got no time for us in the Yard—never did have."

"We shall have to tell Ma about his notice before tomorrow," Iris said. "We can't let her turn up and see it without any warning. She's not going to like it."

"No more am I going to like it," he said. "Grit all over me shell fish!"

They had turned off the High Road into a side street at the end of which was an alley that ran between two large, sombre houses. Through the alley, with its back to one of these houses, lay Lantern Place, an unexpected, tranquil little backwater in which three small terraced houses looked on to a gravelled court. The blank garden walls of the large houses bounded this court, closing it in and leaving only a narrow gap which led through to an open stretch of grass and hawthorn trees beyond.

Two of the terraced houses were in darkness, but the middle one, which belonged to Aunt Camille and Uncle Harry, was all alight and that was where the family was gathered.

3

" ARE you going to tell Ma, or am I?"
Iris asked as they closed the door
behind them.

Uncle Wally pretended not to hear.
"Sounds as though Maurice is there," he
remarked, as he hung up his scarf and hat.

"Yes, but we shall have to tell Ma, just
the same," responded Iris, and she went
into the front room.

Her grandmother, Ascot Tagg, was
sitting in an armchair on one side of the
fireplace and Ma was at the other. Aunt
Camille and Uncle Harry were at the table.
An upright piano stood against the wall
opposite the door and Maurice Royal, the
entertainer, who was looked on as one of
the family, sat perched on the stool with
his back to the keyboard.

"Well, upon my soul!" he exclaimed in
his deep, gritty voice when Iris walked in,
and he edged his way round the table and
hugged her. Then he held her away to get
a better look at her.

"Upon my soul," he said again, "the sight of you does me good, my Iris."

She returned his hug. "Oh, Maurice, how lovely to see you," she said. "How did you manage to get away?"

"Been rehearsing all day and I just got a break. I'm coming again tomorrow," he said.

He was short and fat and he smelt of scented soap and aftershave lotion. He wore a gold ring and a diamond tie pin and he had a red rose in his buttonhole and the material of his dark suit was wonderful. His face was broad, swarthy, ugly and good-humoured. There was a photograph of him on the piano in a silver frame, rather younger but unmistakable. It was the one that always appeared in the Press and on theatre programmes.

"Well, when you two have done exchanging compliments perhaps Iris'll say hallo to her ma and me," said Ascot Tagg. "Come on, let's have a look at you, girl."

"Oh, Gran, I can only say hallo to one at a time," protested Iris. She made her way over to the fireplace, stooping to kiss Uncle Harry on the way. She embraced her grandmother and then sat on the pouffe beside her mother's chair.

"Everything OK, Ma?" she asked softly.

Amelia Arethusa Crockett was dark complexioned and ugly with her gaunt, high-bridged nose; she was gypsyish with her black, oily hair and the great gold hoop ear-rings which Dad had given her. Now she smiled at Iris, took her hand and said in her hoarse voice:

"He sent you his love, dearie." Her eyes had their far-away look.

"Oh, Ma! You gave him mine, didn't you?"

"Of course I did. I was just telling the others he seems a lot better, Iris. Asked after everyone, he did. But I could hardly bear leaving him—Christmas and all!"

Tears began to spill down Melia's face and she shook her head angrily. "He's not idling," she said. "He does lessons—some of the things he missed when he was at school. He'll show us all yet, my Tom will."

"Yes, of course he will, he's got lots of good in him," Iris consoled her.

"Of course he has," Aunt Camille said,

and she squeezed her way into the kitchen which led off the sitting room. "Show Gran your dress while I make some tea," she said.

Iris had to stand on a chair to display the dress, for the room was too crowded for them to get a clear view otherwise, but her pleasure at their approbation was dulled because of the notice board at the Yard.

"I don't like your hair, though," Ascot remarked when they had finished admiring the sheath dress with its jacket and skirt. "The outfit's all right. A bit skimpy. Why don't you have a nice bit of lace at the neck—or a fissue? That'd make all the difference—a nice fissue."

"I'll say it would," said Maurice.

"But, Gran, it's the plain, uncluttered look that makes it," protested Iris.

"Have it your own way. I like something a bit more fancy. Why, I remember the dress Camel made for me the last Ascot I ever went to. That was a dress if you like —none of your two three farthings there!"

She sniffed derisively. Iris found it difficult to imagine her grandmother young and smart, for she had only seen her as an old woman in sombre colours, although her face was round and apple red and she had little twinkling merry blue eyes. She always wore heavy gold ear-rings studded with turquoise and the weight of these had stretched the lobes of her ears to a hideous size. Her hair, which was still black and very sparse, was rolled up on old-fashioned steel curlers which made her look as though she were wearing a helmet. She put the curlers in the moment she got up in the mornings and took them out at tea time, as she found this method so much more comfortable than sleeping in them.

Maurice had turned to the piano and was strumming a tune; Ma was looking into the fire and Uncle Wally was watching her with an anxious look on his face.

Iris knew he was trying to think of a way to break the news about the board and presently he jerked it out all in a jumble of words so that nobody heard what he said the first time.

"What's that?" queried Ascot. "You do mumble these days, Wally. Else I'm going deaf."

"I said there's a notice board gone up

at the Yard today," he repeated gruffly. "Looks like things are moving at last."

"Notice board? What sort of notice board?" demanded Ma, straightening her back. She was suddenly alert, on the defensive.

Maurice stopped strumming and Aunt Camille came to the kitchen door to listen with the teapot in her hands.

"Iris saw it," said Wally accusingly.

"What was on it, then? Come on—tell us, for goodness' sake," appealed Ascot.

Wally looked helplessly at Iris, and she began to tell them about the board, recalling as many of the names as she could, and as she did so the complexity of the planning began to dawn on her and she could feel the immensity of the scheme dwarfing her, diminishing them all and edging them relentlessly out.

"I'd have thought someone would have let us know," Melia said blankly. "I suppose Mr. Redmayne's won his battle with the council, then."

"That's it. He's had that board all ready to hoist up any time this last year, I shouldn't wonder," remarked Uncle Harry.

"If it's all planned and cut and dried how are we going to fare?" Melia asked. "That Redmayne will throw us out as soon as look at us if it suits him."

"Why should he? You've never done him any harm," said Maurice.

"No? He might think different," Melia answered shortly.

Aunt Camille put the teapot down. "Why should he bear malice after all these years?" she asked.

"Because it's his nature," Melia replied. "I can see him now in that boater and Eton suit he used to wear. He used to make horrible faces at me, he did. He called me a dirty little beast."

"Oh, Ma, why?" cried Iris.

"I suppose he thought I was," said Melia. "I remember a time when I'd made a fort out of bits of stone and put a garden in front with orange peel and cauliflower sprigs for flowers. I thought it was lovely. Then along came Master Cyril. 'You dirty little beast,' he said. 'You wait. One day I'll sweep you back into the gutter where you belong. You and all your trash.' And he kicked my fort over."

"Well, what of it? He was only a

schoolboy. He'll have forgotten it,"
Camille said.

"Forgotten the way I kicked his legs?
Not likely. He'd have throttled me if his
father hadn't come by and separated us.
He made us tell him what we were fighting
about and that's the bit he'll never forgive.
Dr. Redmayne told young Cyril he was to
treat me just as kind as though I was his
sister and that needled him far worse than
a good hiding would have done. I bet he
remembers it, just the same as I do."

"Here, for goodness' sake give us a cup
of tea!" cried Ascot. "You're a proper
elephant, Melia. Never forget, do you? I
was there when Dr. Redmayne died,
wasn't I? There was only young Cyril and
me in the room and his old dad looked at
him so kind and gentle. 'You won't turn
my sparrows out of my Yard when I'm
gone, will you, Cyril?' he asked. That's
enough for you, isn't it?"

"There's nothing in writing though,"
Melia objected. "It's all on trust."

"That's the way it's always been," Ascot
said. "Young Cyril was very cut up that
day, I can tell you. He sort of gulped and
said, 'No Father, I won't.' And then he

42

stood there looking out of the window at the Yard."

"Pity we don't know what he was thinking," remarked Wally.

"I expect he was thinking of his dad. I know I was," Ascot said, and her face was gentle as she recalled their old friend and her mention of him brought a quietness for they had all known and loved him.

"Getting on time for me to go, Camel," warned Harry presently, nudging her elbow as she stood by his side at the table.

"I was forgetting," Camille said, and she fetched his mac from the hall and looked out to see if the sky was still clear and the Yard was forgotten in the flurry of his departure.

Harry Merritt played the fiddle and he had been in the orchestra at the Piazza Theatre ever since *The Silver Staircase* began its phenomenal run. People often asked when young Reub Hillstein, who had written the book and lyrics of the show, was going to give them another and Harry always replied that he could afford to take his time.

After he had gone Maurice began to make Wally and Ascot laugh: he imitated people in the audience at his last cabaret show and Ascot shouted with mirth. Ma was laughing, too. Then suddenly Iris saw it was not laughter but tears. Melia's dark eyes were glittering with them and they were running down her face, streaking through the powder and falling on to her lap.

"Ma," she said, putting her arms round her. "Ma darling. Is it because of the notice?"

"No," Melia sobbed. "It's so nice and cosy here with the fire and everything."

They all knew she was thinking of Tom.

"Just leave me alone," she said. "There, dearie, I'm fine. I'm fine." Somehow she got rid of the tears and spoke in a determined tone.

"I'm a fool to get upset over the Yard and that Cyril," she said. "Ascot's right. If he promised his dad he'd leave us alone then he will and people can say what they like."

"Let's think the best of him till we know the worst," said Maurice. "Come on —'For He's a Jolly Good Fellow'!"

He struck massive chords and they all joined in the chorus and gradually the

44

shock of hearing about the notice board at the Yard subsided.

But every time Iris thought of it a chill came over her and she could not forget the man in the Rolls either. Cyril Redmayne! She could almost see him kicking a child's fort over, flaring out his nostrils and narrowing his steely eyes. It scarcely seemed possible that he was the son of the dear old doctor with his lovely white hair and his warm friendly hands that she had slipped hers into so confidently whenever she saw him in the Yard.

Well, tomorrow she was going to help at the stall and perhaps she would see Cyril Redmayne again. Perhaps the lamplight had been cruel to him. He might look kindlier by day.

4

THAT Christmas Saturday was a day in a million. There was a frosty sparkle in the air, but all day the sky was clear and at noon, in sheltered places, the sun was almost warm.

Trade was brisk in Sparrow's Yard and old Ascot Tagg had come to help at the stall. Her actions were slow and deliberate, she never allowed herself to be rushed and she always gave extra weight tossing in another potato when the scales had already gone down heavily.

"Watch it, Gran. You'll ruin us if you go on like that," Iris said.

Ascot winked at her. "You want 'em to come back, don't you, girl?" she asked.

"More spuds here, Wally," shouted Melia in her hoarse voice. "Another crate of toms while you're about it."

Uncle Wally was bustling backwards and forwards from the storage shed, replenishing the stall as fast as he could go and muttering to himself under his breath.

"How am I to get me cockles and whelks dished out?" he worried as he tipped the potatoes out. "It's all right for you, but what about me?"

Uncle Wally described his Saturdays as "all go", for besides helping Melia he ran a shell-fish stall which he set up under the chestnut tree in the middle of the Yard at midday. Then, in the evenings, he took it to the Duke's Head, where he did a roaring trade while Melia and her friends sat in the bar at their ease.

"I'm still on me trotters when you're all nicely sat," he complained crossly as he pushed Iris aside to tip out some more sprouts.

"Never mind, it's a lovely long Christmas," she said.

She was in her element when she served at the stall and her spirits always rose. Six of Edwards, one of onions, one of carrots and the greens are lovely! Nobby sprouts, shining white leeks and tight, buttony cauliflowers!

"Nice to see old Mrs. Tagg looking so well," the customers remarked.

"Not so much of the old," cried Ascot jauntily.

"This is a tonic to her," rejoiced Melia, and she told Iris not to remark when Ascot gave too much change, as she frequently did.

"She's quite a draw," Melia said. "Everyone's glad to see old Ascot can still lend a hand and it does me good to have her here." When Ascot was at the stall Melia always had the unreasonable but comfortable feeling that not much could go wrong in Villa Park.

Dinner time seemed to come extraordinarily quickly that day and Melia and Ascot went to theirs first. At home Camille would have a good hot stew waiting for them and the fire would be glowing red. From her centre house in Lantern Place she unobtrusively controlled the other two, conjuring up meals when they were wanted and seeing that the fires did not fall low.

Iris had not thought about Cyril Redmayne all the morning and there was no sign of any activity behind the neglected hedge. Gran was right. There was nothing for them to worry about. She waved cheerfully to Mrs. Tilley at her fruit stall on the other side and Mrs. Tilley waved back and said something to Alfie, who was helping her. Presently he came over to Iris with a beaker of cocoa.

"Have a drop of drink, Iris," he said. "Keep the cold out."

"I'm all in a gorgeous glow now," she said, "but the cocoa's lovely."

"Mum always makes it good," Alfie said. "Lucky they didn't start pulling the house down before Christmas, eh? It won't half make a mess when they do."

"I expect it will," she agreed.

He waited while she drank because he meant to take the beaker back and drink out of the same side as she had done. He was eight years older than Iris and he loved her. He had been her faithful admirer from the time she had made her first appearance in Sparrow's Yard as a baby in arms and if he ever married anyone it was going to be Iris. She had no idea, he thought, how much he had enjoyed giving her those secret driving lessons, just sitting beside her and putting his hand over hers on the steering wheel now and then.

Alfie's chief worry was his father, who would never walk again and had to be pushed about in a wheelchair, and this curtailed his own freedom. Now that Iris was at Abbeyfield there was also a lurking fear that someone from the world outside the Yard would find her and take her away from him.

"I was thinking about next Tuesday," he remarked. "What about going up west and doing a flick?"

"I can't manage it that day," she said. "One of the girls at college has asked me to her place and I promised to go."

"Oh." His spirits fell so low at this that the whole complexion of the day changed. "Then another time?" he asked.

"Yes, of course another time. I'd like to, Alfie."

"OK, then. You've got a customer coming."

He felt unutterably depressed when he left her and he saw with disfavour that her customer was a young man and a good-looking one, but he did not know that he was Cyril Redmayne's son.

Iris did not know who her customer was either. She only knew that she had seen him reading a score in the train the night before; she only knew that now he was near her the world was standing still. Now he wore casual clothes and he looked even more attractive while she was in her dingy working gear. She could not see the vegetables her hands were touching, she could only feel their cold shapes. Her eyes met his and it was as though the whole earth was listening and the flowers on Princess Potter's stall stiffened to attention. But why did he gaze at her as though he half expected her and the stall to rise in the air and vanish out of sight?

Johnny Redmayne had come to see his grandfather's old house before it was demolished, but his first sight of Sparrow's Yard put it out of his mind for the pulsing, vibrant personality of the place came to him so strongly that he was engulfed by it.

The colours, the smells and the sounds excited him and throbbed in his mind like the beat of a drum. Here was music, or at least the makings of it, and he stood still almost expecting to hear a burst of sound.

He noticed the stalls—the Cheeks' salad stall, the Tilleys' fruit and Princess Potter's flowers. Then he saw Iris Crockett for the first time and it was a moment he never forgot for the rest of his life.

It was as though everything of beauty in that Yard, every good emotion, every expression of love and kindness that had ever been there, crystallized into a seed that took root in him that instant and began to grow. She was looking at him, too. She had seen him, really seen him, with a strange but unmistakable sort of recognition which puzzled him. He did not know that she had seen him in the train the night before and had wondered about him and wished that he would look her way.

Now she was waiting for him to ask for something and he had no idea what to say. But he must speak—he couldn't just stand there.

"A pound of Brussels sprouts, please," he said.

She scooped them into the scales, weighed them and asked: "Have you a basket—or shall I put them in a bag for you?"

"May I have a bag, please?" he said.

It was a plain, brown paper bag. He took it and handed her the money and she gave him some change out of her leather apron pocket. But that couldn't be all. He had to say something else—something worth while.

"Are you Amelia Crockett?" he asked.

She laughed. "No, I'm Iris," she said. "That's my mother's name."

"I just wondered. I'm new to this place. I mean we've only just moved here." Usually he could speak to a girl quite easily, but this one was different.

"What's it like here?" he asked.

"It's home to me and I think it's wonderful," she said. "The streets are not very much, but there's the Villa. I expect you've seen that?"

"I didn't even know there was one!"

"Oh, but that's the whole thing about Villa Park!" she exclaimed. "It's right at the centre and everything radiates from it. Can't you imagine? Mile upon mile of orchards in an enormous circle with the Villa in the middle like the heart of a flower!"

"Orchards?" he repeated.

"Oh, there I go!" she laughed. "That was years ago, but there are times now when you can half close your eyes and believe it's still as it used to be."

She paused and then went on: "There are still old fruit trees miles from the Villa where you'd never expect to see them. That chestnut tree there is an old villa tree. When there were millions and millions of them just think how the air must have smelt! And the petals. Why, they must have lain as thick as snow!"

Her eyes were shining and her face was bright and the sun was on her hair.

"You make it sound wonderful," he said.

"You should go there in the early morning when there aren't many people about."

"Is that when you go?"

"If I can. I like it best in early spring just before the leaves are out. You know, when the branches look gold and tawny with the buds. Sometimes in March you get wonderful days."

"I can't wait till March," he said.

"Oh well, you don't have to. You can go any day."

"Maybe you'll show me round sometime?"

Suddenly she wondered if she had been talking too much, rattling on to a complete stranger as though she had known him all her life.

"Please," he said.

"Well, one day perhaps."

"Tomorrow?"

"It's Christmas tomorrow! After the holiday."

"Shall I find you here?"

"I expect so. There now, I must serve this lady. Excuse me, please."

A woman had pushed her way between them and she began to reel off a list of vegetables in an indignant tone as though she resented their conversation. Several other women began to line up behind her and Johnny saw he would not be able to speak to Iris any more. He stood back uncertainly, feeling he ought to go yet unable to tear himself away.

There was a stable behind the stall and a short, elderly man was leading out a horse to which was harnessed a mobile stall painted white, red and gold. It had a sky-blue canopy and a sign proclaimed the owner to be Wally Tagg who sold shell fish straight from the ocean bed.

Wally Tagg! There was five foot six of him and he wore a red choker, but the sight of him struck a note in Johnny's brain and he knew there must be music to convey the pugnacity and grit and lurking humour of Wally Tagg.

"Be with you in a minute, Iris," called Wally.

"It's all right, Uncle Wally. I can manage," she said.

Johnny supposed he had better move away, but if only he could speak to her properly! It was impossible now, for the crowd at the stall was thickening. Reluctantly he strolled into the High Road, looking back for a last glimpse of her.

Somehow it was unbelievable to find a girl like this serving vegetables. She was beautiful—lovely. Her face was delicate with its fine skin and she had wonderful dark eyes that were neither green nor grey but something between the two. It didn't seem right that she should be in the open weighing up potatoes and cabbages, for she lacked the toughness of the other people in the Yard. Yet she must be one of them. She had called the old man Uncle Wally and her mother owned the stall.

Johnny found himself wandering along the road clutching the bag full of sprouts. What was he to do with them? Outside a butcher's he paused beside a dumpy little woman with a trolley basket who was gazing intently at the turkeys strung up outside. She was completely absorbed. He dropped his bag of sprouts into her basket and she turned like a viper.

"Here, what's the idea? Dumping your rubbish in my basket! I never did, indeed. You take that bag out of my basket or I'll call a copper."

"I—I'm sorry," spluttered Johnny. "It's only some sprouts I don't really want."

His face was scarlet and people were looking at him as he stood there awkwardly clutching the bag which had got damp through contact with something wet in the basket. It began to disintegrate and the bright, nobby sprouts fell to the ground scattering in all directions.

"Oh, shame. Poor young fellow."

"Here, I've got another bag. Pop 'em in here."

"Don't worry, duck. You won't lose none."

He was grasping a sprout in each hand and suddenly he felt like a Colossus standing there above the bending, groping women who seemed to be intent on retrieving every single sprout. The woman with the trolley basket was still staring at him suspiciously.

"Here," he said, thrusting the two sprouts into her hands, "You hold these. I've got a plane to catch."

Before she could protest he was away, sprinting through the crowds and laughing at the ridiculous situation he had got himself into. And all for Iris! A girl he didn't even know.

Oh, but she was worth it. She was the one he was laughing for, sprinting for. He was in front of a florist's now. "I must give her flowers," he thought, flowers for Iris, carpets and carpets of flowers for Iris.

But discretion called for something small. Not a bouquet, just a token. He left the shop with a little cellophane box containing three pink rose buds on a bed of moss. Now all he had to do was to present them and if he waited till closing time she might allow him to see her home.

When he returned to the stall Iris was

no longer there. A woman he took to be Amelia Crockett was in charge. Could she ever have looked like Iris? She was serving fast and he could not get a good view of her because her face was shadowed by a woollen scarf which she wore tied under her chin. He waited a long time, watching and hoping Iris might come back. It was almost dark. She was not coming any more. He did not know what to do and he felt rather desperate. Mrs. Crockett was beginning to pack up.

He screwed up his courage and approached her. "Excuse me, but will Iris be coming back?" he asked.

Amelia Crockett looked up at him and he saw her full face for the first time. He thought she looked forbidding and she eyed him hard.

"Iris has gone home," she said. "What do you want her for?"

"Then would you be kind enough to give her these?" he asked, holding out the box of roses.

She glanced down at it and her expression changed. She could never have looked like Iris but there was something in her weather-beaten face that moved him in a queer sort of way. He did not know what it was except that it was something that Iris had too. It was disturbing because he thought Mrs. Crockett looked as though she had suffered a great deal.

Now, to his relief, she was smiling, and it was a quick, lively smile.

"Lovely," she said. "But wouldn't you rather give it to her yourself? Know the way? Straight along the High Road, second on the left and through the alley to Lantern Place. You can't miss it."

"Oh, thank you very much," he said. "I'll go there right away."

Melia chuckled. "Give her half an hour," she said, "she'll be cleaning up."

He thanked her and wandered away. The thought of Iris made Villa Park a place of enchantment and suddenly the tune that had been in his mind when he first saw Sparrow's Yard was back again, only now it was linked with her and he had to make something unforgettable of the union.

There was a bench circling the chestnut tree, so he sat there to note down the tune. He felt in harmony with his surroundings and he remembered, almost with disbelief, that his father had given him a very different picture of the place.

"A rough old paved square with an overgrown tree in the middle and a few shabby stalls," his father had called it. For Johnny it was a magnificent conglomeration of life and colour and sound and he had an intense longing to capture and distil the essence of it. The tune that had been haunting him was part of it, but only a part.

"Lovely celery, almond celery, all crisp!"

The cry was harsh and lusty in the gathering dusk and the woman who uttered it looked like a picture by Hogarth. Her coarse paisley scarf was tied round her head in gypsy fashion and the ends were streaming down her back.

At the fruit stall Mrs. Tilley was beginning to pack up. She wore a black felt hat garlanded with sprays of woollen flowers and her fitted coat had a fur collar and it did not accord with the trousers and stout boots which completed her ensemble. Her face was pale and solemn and she had large, gold-rimmed spectacles.

"It's the feel of the place," Johnny

thought. "That's what I've got to capture. Somehow. Somehow."

He felt restless because of his need to express his feelings in the only way he knew—in music. And suddenly an idea came to him, a bold, rousing idea which caught his imagination and swept him away in the first flood of excitement. There was no denying the soul of Sparrow's Yard and Johnny hoped with all his heart that it was strong enough and fighting enough to preserve itself when his father's office block rose storeys high from the ruins of Dr. Redmayne's house.

5

LANTERN PLACE was illuminated by a single old-fashioned gas lamp and its gentle glow lent a special charm to the three houses.

Johnny went to the middle one, as the other two were in darkness, but now he was there he felt like an intruder. He waited uncomfortably, half wishing he had not knocked. Then the door was opened by a very slight, dainty little woman who reminded him irresistibly of the fairy godmother in a pantomime standing on tiptoe and extending a wand.

"There, I said I heard someone coming through the alley!" she cried in a tone of triumph as though his arrival had clinched an argument. She smiled at him encouragingly and he held out the roses and stammered something. She peered at the box and then looked at him again, more closely this time.

"Why, I do declare I saw you in the train from Abbeyfield last night and you were reading a score," she said.

"That's right, I was. *The Silver Staircase*," he replied.

"You don't say! Well, you've come to the right house. My husband's in the orchestra at the Piazza—has been ever since it started."

Her blue eyes twinkled and she read the card which he had written at the florist's: *Iris—from Johnny*.

"Are you Johnny?" she asked. "Then do come in and I'll tell Iris."

She left him in the hall and he was aware of a steep staircase rising in front of him, of hooks on the wall, of a shabby mac suspended from one of them and a rather dashing soft black trilby perched on another. The next moment Iris was there and she had his roses in her hand.

She looked as though she did not believe her eyes when she saw him, but she was smiling and the sight of her was wonderful.

"However did you know where I lived?" she asked.

"Your mother told me. You don't mind, do you?"

Mind! She had been thinking of him all the afternoon and wishing she had made a date to show him the Villa. It was not often a second chance came so easily. But to think Ma had come home and never said a word!

She looked down at the roses and her face was soft.

"Lovely," she murmured. "They're lovely. Thank you—Johnny."

He would have liked to watch her with her head bent over the flowers for a long time, but the little woman who had opened the door came into the hall again and said: "Do bring your friend in, dear. I'm just going to make some tea. We're all gasping."

"All right, Aunt Camille," Iris said. "Can you stay for a little while, Johnny?"

"Rather," he said.

She felt as though her feet were not quite touching the ground. His name was Johnny and already he belonged and because of him it was as though she saw Aunt Camille's sitting room for the first time with the Turkey carpet and ruby chenille tablecloth covered by the lace one that her aunt had made during her years of touring as a conjuror's assistant. There were white swan vases on top of the piano and sea shells on the mantelpiece and innumerable photographs on the walls, some of them were so old that their good-will messages were only just decipherable.

Ascot was in her usual chair by the fire, but this evening she wore her best maroon velvet dress that covered her feet and hid her carpet slippers. Her hair was set in stiffly rolled curls on either side of a wide parting and her fingers glittered with diamond half-hoops.

Maurice, in whose honour she had dressed herself so elaborately, was at the table like a schoolboy waiting for his tea.

"Well, we met before, didn't we," said Ma, coming forward with a smile as Johnny followed her in. "Maybe Iris will introduce us properly now."

"This is Johnny," Iris said.

Ascot held out her hand. "Just Johnny? Nothing more?" she chuckled.

"Johnny Redmayne," he said as Iris hesitated. He took Ascot's hand.

"Redmayne?" she repeated.

"Yes."

He noticed the almost imperceptible

66

pause, and then Ma spoke and there was an edge to her voice.

"Do you belong to the family that owns Sparrow's Yard?" she asked.

"My grandfather lived there once," he said. "Now it belongs to my father."

"I took you for a boy from Abbeyfield Tech," said Ma. "I'd no idea you were a Redmayne. Iris never said she knew you."

The soft look had left Iris's face; she looked startled, almost frightened, he thought.

"That's my fault," he said quickly. "I didn't introduce myself properly. I've got into an awful casual way."

"Well, it doesn't matter, does it?" said Maurice in his deep humorous voice. "It's nice to know you, Johnny. Are you new to Villa Park, then?"

"Yes, we've just moved here from Abbeyfield, but my father lived here when he was a boy," said Johnny, grateful to be accepted by this man whose face was so strangely familiar to him.

"Why bless my soul, it's the old doctor all over again!" exclaimed Ascot. "Let's have another look at you. Same voice—same hair. My word, I never would have believed it, would you, Camel? Come and shake hands with me again, Johnny. Your grandfather was a special friend of mine."

Her warm voice dispelled the embarrassment which Melia's sharpness had created and Johnny sat beside her and he was soon talking to her as though he had known her from his cradle up. At first Melia was quiet but Camille and Maurice made up for her.

Iris was still recovering from the shock and when Aunt Camille went into the kitchen she followed her.

"I hadn't a clue he was a Redmayne," she whispered. "And he said Ma asked him to call. She must be mad now."

"What's in a name? Redmaynes can probably be as nice as other people. I think it's very lucky getting to know him."

"Ma won't like him, though."

"Well, I do. On sight. I'm never wrong," Aunt Camille said. "I can pick out the true ones from a mile off and he's a true one, Iris. You may be sure of that."

She handed Iris two plates of bridge rolls and said:

"Take them in, ducky. You look as though you are going to start juggling with them."

Iris found it difficult to collect her thoughts. When she returned to the sitting room she saw that Johnny and Ascot were still deep in conversation and he looked completely at home. Ma got up to help with the table and they bore in dishes of shrimps and prawns, a whole ham, jars of pickles and chutneys, an apple tart and a huge cake.

"Come along now, gather round," Camille said, as she made her last trip from the kitchen. "Not you, Ascot. You stay there, where you're comfortable."

"So long as you don't forget to look after me," Ascot said.

Aunt Camille sat at the head of the table and Johnny and Iris eased their way into seats on either side of her, which left Ma at the far end where she could attend to Ascot's needs.

Maurice was next to Johnny and he sharpened the carving knife and tackled the ham and Ascot sat back and surveyed the preparations critically.

"Well, Johnny and I have had a nice old chat," she said. "Glad to see you didn't forget the shrimps, Camel. Remember how Dr. Redmayne used to enjoy our shrimp teas?"

"That I do," Camel said.

"You've made me wish I'd known my grandfather more than ever," Johnny said.

"I suppose you'll be a doctor too?" asked Ascot.

"No, I'm not made that way. I wanted to take up music, but I'm not all that good and Dad was so sure I'd be wasting my time I had to get a job in a bank. Still, we've a good operatic society and that's a help," he said.

"What do you do—sing?" asked Maurice.

"Play the piano mostly," Johnny said. "There's always someone who wants an accompanist."

"You must hate working in a bank when you want to study music, though," remarked Camille, "I'm sure I should."

"I suppose I know my limitations," said Johnny. "And I'm terribly lucky to be in the Foreign Department—it's a good place to be."

"Maybe you'll have a spell abroad sometime, then?" said Maurice.

"Not a chance of that," Johnny

answered. "As far as I'm concerned abroad is strictly for holidays."

"And we shan't be thinking of those for a bit," Camille said.

They finished eating and when Camille had cleared the table she suggested pushing it back to give room round the piano so that they could have a sing-song.

"That's what we like to do after our tea, Johnny," she said. "Just a few of the old chestnuts. What do you say?"

"But that's only when we're by ourselves!" cried Iris. "Goodness, we all sing like tom cats."

"Speak for yourself," said Ascot.

"There's nothing I like better than a bit of home-made music," Johnny said. "I'm all for it."

"Shall I play or will you, Maurice?" asked Camille.

"You," he said. "Let me have a nice listen for a change."

Camille took off her rings, massaged her hands like a concert pianist and struck an impressive chord, followed by an arpeggio. Then she went into an old song— "Lavender, Sweet Lavender".

"This is Ascot's song," she told Johnny. "Come on, Ascot, sing up."

From her seat by the fireside Ascot took up the old air. Melia and Camille both joined in and Iris sang softly, stealing a glance at Johnny to see how he was taking it. His face was serious and intent and there was no hint of a smile. He was enjoying it.

Melia sang "My Old Man Said Follow the Van" with the rhythm and timing of the music-hall performer. She made them all want to join in the chorus and they sang with gusto. Then Camille sang "I Dreamt I Dwelt in Marble Halls" in a rather sweet little voice.

Johnny found himself listening contentedly; it was so pleasant and so different from anything he had known. This was an entirely new kind of enjoyment to him and it gave him the feeling he had sometimes had when he was in the house alone with his piano.

Now it was Iris's turn. She sang "The Last Rose of Summer", and he listened entranced. She stood with one hand on Aunt Camille's shoulder and the candlelight fell on her face. The other hand strayed to his roses which she had pinned to her dress. He told himself he would never lose the picture of her as she was now and he longed to touch her and to make her aware of him, yet he knew that to disturb her would be to destroy the picture, for she was lost in the song.

When she finished she turned to him and said: "Now it's you, Johnny. What are you going to sing?"

"Gosh, I never sing to be heard!" he exclaimed. "Not even in my bath."

"But you must sing something," said Ascot. "We all take a turn."

"No excuses," added Camille.

A sudden impulse made him say: "All right. But I'll have to play this one myself. It's new and you won't know it."

Camille moved off the piano stool and he took her place. "I'm afraid I only know the opening words," he said.

He began to play the theme tune of his new song. He knew the words would go something like "The Old Songs, the Sweet Songs", but he didn't know any more. This was the first time he had played to people who listened and they were all listening, especially Maurice Royal.

He had an easy touch and he felt a special pleasure in playing this song on Camille's old upright piano. There was something right about it. When he finished Iris said, "Oh, don't stop—do play the rest of it."

"I wish I could," he said.

Camille had been watching him attentively. "Johnny, did you compose that?" she asked.

He nodded.

"I thought so," she said with a smile, and she glanced at Maurice, who shook his head slightly as though he did not wish to be drawn in.

"Well—it's a sort of hobby," Johnny said apologetically.

"Composing music a hobby? I think it's something much more exciting than that," Iris said. "I think it's wonderful. Auntie, just think! A composer— here! Just where he's appreciated."

"A composer—me? Holy smoke—I just catch on to jingling tunes," Johnny protested.

"I should call that haunting more than jingling," Melia remarked, and Ascot agreed with her.

"I think it's lovely," Iris said. "It makes me feel sort of—I don't know. Play it again, Johnny, will you?"

So he played it again and Iris sat beside him stealing soft glances at him because it was so wonderful to think that he had really composed this tune. It made her want to say words of praise, but she could only think over and over again: "Oh, Johnny, oh, Johnny!" and experience the inexplicable thrill of being near him.

He went on playing and gave them some of the other songs he had written and Camille and Ascot's faces were serene and happy as they listened. Melia was lost in her own thoughts and she could not enjoy herself as the others did. She appreciated the music as much as they did but she could not forget that Johnny was Cyril Redmayne's son.

Maurice seemed to be dozing, but when Johnny left the piano he took his place and began to strum in an absent-minded manner. After a bit he went on to play in the style that had kept him to the fore as an entertainer for so many years. He played through old-time favourites and went on to present-day hits and then, almost magically it seemed, they found themselves listening to a medley of Johnny's tunes.

Iris's lips formed an ecstatic "Oh" of delight and Camille's eyes danced and Ascot nodded her approval. Johnny looked bewildered. He was only just beginning to gather who Maurice was and now he could scarcely believe that his favourite disc artist was playing the songs he had composed and embellishing them with his own variations.

Maurice played "The Old Songs" last and then he twisted round on the stool and said: "You should get a good lyric for that. It's not a bad little number. I know a boy who might be able to help you."

"Do you? That would be marvellous!" Johnny exclaimed. "I'm always stuck for words."

"You want to get the words sorted out. They're important," Maurice remarked with a grin.

Not long afterwards he said he must go, and he offered Johnny a lift which was accepted. In the general commotion of farewells and Christmas wishes Johnny

76

found no chance to arrange a further meeting with Iris.

"You must come again," Camille said.

"I should like to," he answered.

Melia did not echo the invitation, but Ascot did.

"I'll see you after Christmas," he said to Iris, and he hoped that the touch of his hand thrilled her as much as hers did him.

She felt miserable as soon as the door closed behind him and she went back into the sitting room to find Ma looking troubled and Ascot chuckling to herself.

"No one ever gave me roses when I served 'em a pound of sprouts," she teased. "When I was young all I ever got was a bit of fried fish or a screw of chips as a love token."

"Who's talking about love?" demanded Melia gruffly.

"I am," said Ascot.

"Then don't. Don't go putting ideas into her head," said Melia, giving Iris a hard look. "That boy's a Redmayne and don't you forget it. He's not for us."

"Why, whatever do you mean?" asked Iris.

"I mean he's his father's son and we

don't want any truck with him. That Cyril Redmayne wouldn't touch one of us with the end of a barge pole. Not even you, Iris. So he'll soon put a stop to any friendship between you and that son of his. You mark my words."

Iris stared at her mother and her lip began to tremble.

"I don't see why . . ." she began.

"You ask Ascot, then. I told you Cyril Redmayne hated us, but I didn't tell you why. It's because his mother ran away when he was a kid. She said she couldn't stand us lot in her front garden with our stalls and the doctor wouldn't turn us out. That's the truth, isn't it, Ascot?"

"The doctor's wife didn't care tuppence for him. All she wanted was to see us in the gutter, but he stuck to his principles. He wasn't having any," Ascot returned.

"I reckon that Cyril will see us in the gutter yet, in spite of his promises," Melia affirmed. "And if you go getting friendly with that boy of his, Iris, you'll just stir him up. I'm warning you. You put that boy right out of your head."

Iris looked from one of them to the other. Her mother's face was tense and

Ascot was sitting with her hands on her knees and an obstinate expression in her eyes.

"You know I'm right, Ascot," Melia accused her.

"I reckon young Johnny takes after his grandfather in more than looks," she retorted. "He's not a bit like his dad. We had a real good evening till you spoilt it, Melia."

"I only spoke for Iris's good," protested Melia.

"Well, I hate people who speak for other people's good. You've only upset her, look! Leave the kids alone. They can fight it out between them if they want to."

"Do you think I'd have asked him round if I'd known who he was?" asked Melia, and she gave a short laugh. "Now that he's seen us in all our glory he's not likely to call again," she said. "I expect he thinks we're dirt, the same as his father does."

"Oh, how can you?" cried Iris. "He's not like that, I know he isn't!"

Melia set her mouth grimly and Iris felt as though a heavy stone had been planted in her chest. Suppose her mother were

79

right and he didn't ever call again? She could scarcely bear the thought, and yet how crazy it was to be so perturbed about someone she had spoken to for the first time only a few hours before.

Aunt Camille was in the kitchen beginning to wash up and Iris went to help her. They did not speak, but it was a sympathetic silence and when they finished Aunt Camille asked her if she would like to put her roses in the refrigerator.

"They'll last better in there," she said.

Iris unpinned them from her dress reluctantly.

"Don't you worry, my ducky," Aunt Camille said gently. "They'll keep. You see."

6

AUNT CAMILLE'S words proved prophetic, for the flowers were still fresh when Iris went to Caroline's party. The Goldings lived at Abbeyfield and when she found their house she was abashed by the size of it. She felt unsettled and restless because she longed to see Johnny again and she was still too upset by her mother's attitude towards him to feel in the mood for a party.

Caroline opened the door and welcomed her enthusiastically.

"I'm so glad you're here," she said, "come along up to my room and dump your coat."

She started up the wide staircase and Iris followed, her hand resting on the broad balustrade. Caroline looked so pretty and so at home in her luxurious surroundings that Iris felt a stab of jealousy. She was a fish out of water here. Why hadn't she stayed at home, nice and cosy in their own house, or else popping into Auntie Camille's for a cup of tea and a look through the album with the faded press cuttings? Better still, she could have gone to the Villa in the faint hope of seeing Johnny there.

"I'll put those roses in your hair," Caroline was saying, and she led Iris into her bedroom and made her sit at the dressing table while she fixed them in place. "There, what do you think of that?" she asked.

"My!" exclaimed Iris, "It's very sophisticated."

"Isn't it just? Come on, let's go down."

She led the way, chattering all the time, and they entered an enormous room which stretched from the front to the back of the house. One end had been cleared for dancing and the other was furnished as a drawing-room, but there were so many people that Iris only caught brief, tantalizing glimpses of the exquisite furnishings.

Mrs. Golding came to greet her, raising her voice above the din of voices and music, and Caroline was snatched away to dance. Iris felt bemused by the size of the place and by the babble. Mrs. Golding wore black and she looked so easy, so sure of herself and so kind. Her face was smooth and pretty, just like Caroline's, her nails were varnished rose-pink to match her lips.

Suddenly Iris felt she wanted to run out into the open air and race back to Sparrow's Yard for all she was worth and shout at the top of her voice, "Lettuce, lovely lettuce, all fresh," like the Cheek sisters did. Mrs. Golding was just a marionette and she had strings to make her smile and when she talked a little machine enunciated set phrases. She could not feel, she hadn't ever been cold, she could no more hump a sack of potatoes than Ma could stand among all these people and look like one of them. Her feet were probably as fine as her hands. Ma's were hard and horny through standing on the cold stones with an old sack for a rug.

"Here's someone wanting you to do the twist, dear, so I won't keep you talking."

Mrs. Golding's voice seemed to come from a long way off. She was gently propelling her guest towards a tall boy in cream-coloured jeans and a bright blue shirt.

"Johnny!"

"Gosh! Iris!" he exclaimed. "Is it really you?"

He gazed at her incredulously and then took her hands in his. He glanced at the roses in her hair and then looked into her eyes and she was the only one in the room for him.

Mrs. Golding beamed as though she had just brought off a particularly difficult conjuring trick. "Well, how nice. You know each other already," she said in a benevolent tone, and she merged into the moving background of people with a skill that added a further touch of magic to their meeting.

"I wondered if I'd ever see you again," Iris said.

"I knew I'd see you, but I never thought it would be here. What do you say to skipping the twist? There's room to breathe over the other side of the floor and we can talk."

They found a seat in a window alcove and he said: "I've been kicking myself all over Christmas because we didn't make a real date. I very nearly called round yesterday, only I didn't like to butt in so soon."

The heavy weight which had been dragging Iris down lifted miraculously. "I wish you had come," she said. "The house was packed almost solid with friends from the Yard and Uncle Wally sang 'Any Old Iron'. You'd have loved it."

"I guess it was great. We had a very prosaic Christmas."

"You can imagine the squash. Do you know that when Caroline opened the door to me just now I was quite petrified by the sight of so much space? But the minute I saw you I felt fine."

"That's the nicest thing you could say. I hope you'll always feel fine when you see me."

"It's funny the way some people make you feel at home straight off," she said.

"I don't know about feeling at home. You did something very odd to me on Saturday," he said. "Crash, bang and echoing chords. I haven't been right since. But I can't get you straight. You were a stunner in the old duffel coat with your hair down. You were lovely at Lantern

Place and now you're simply wonderful with your hair piled up."

"I expect I'm most natural in the duffel coat," she said thoughtfully. "I feel rather a fraud here. I'm at Abbeyfield Tech with Caroline, but I'm rather an impostor there too, especially as I may not finish the course."

"Why? Too stodgy?"

"No. It's just that Ma might need help with the stall soon. Uncle Wally's getting old and his horse ought to be drawing its pension. So I've learned to drive—no one else in the family can. I still have to pass the test but Alfie says it's in the bag."

"Who's Alfie?"

"Alfie Tilley from the fruit stall. He's been teaching me. Of course, Ma doesn't know—she'd flay me if she did." She paused for a moment and then said, "Why am I telling you all this, Johnny?"

"Because you want me to know," he said.

"I don't generally tell anyone."

"I appreciate it all the more," he replied. He took her hand and his touch filled her with a confidence she had never known before. She felt as though she had found the one with whom she could brave the whole world. He was the one person she wanted to be with and she knew her first impression of him was not going to change.

"Iris, why was your mother so upset when she heard who I was?" he asked.

In the joy of meeting him again she had forgotten her mother's fears but now she was in the midst of them once more.

"She thinks your father will object to us being friends," she said.

"Oh, so that's it. I'm quite sure he couldn't help liking you. There he is now."

The music had come to an end, the energetic contortions of the dancers reached an unwilling halt and the floor cleared. Iris followed Johnny's eyes and saw a tall man with thinning hair watching them from the other side of the room.

The sight of him took her back to the evening when she saw the notice at Sparrow's Yard for the first time and as he looked at her from across the room she thought of Ma and a wave of indignation swept over her.

"Come over and meet him," Johnny said. "I won't let him eat you."

"I'm sure he wouldn't want to," she said. "Ma could be right, Johnny. It makes a difference—me belonging to the Yard, I mean."

"What's wrong with the Yard? I fell in love with it the moment I saw it," he said. "Finding you there makes me sure I wasn't wrong about it."

She could not refuse to meet his father, but as she crossed the floor she wished once again that she could turn and run home and crowd round the fire with Ma and Gran and Aunt Camille. Instead here she was looking up into the cold face of Cyril Redmayne, while inside her a weak little voice cried out in protest: "Please let it be a mistake! Don't let Johnny belong to you!"

But there was no mistake. At the same time Mr. Redmayne was not nearly as fearsome as Ma had led her to think. He was not in the least like Johnny—his features were more regular. His manners were courteous and if she had not known who he was he might have seemed as pleasant as Mr. Golding.

"You have nothing to drink," he remarked after a moment. "Come along, Johnny. Do your stuff and fetch Iris a glass of something and while you're about it you can bring me a light sherry."

"I'd like some coke," she said.

"Nothing stronger than that? I thought all you girls drank gin," Mr. Redmayne remarked.

She felt as though she were alone with him in a great echoing void now that Johnny had left them.

"I've never had it," she said. "Only brandy in milk sometimes and I don't like that."

"Extraordinary. And refreshing, too. You look such a young woman of the world, though. Tell me, did I see you at Villa Park the other evening, or am I mistaken?"

"No. You were driving out of Sparrow's Yard and I was on my way home from Abbeyfield Tech," she said.

"That's a very long journey for you, surely?"

"Yes, but it's the only place for the dress course I'm doing and I don't mind travelling."

"Was it Caroline who gave you that attractive hair-do?" he asked with a smile.

"Yes. She's a real wizard at it."

"I like the roses. And did you design the dress you're wearing?"

"Well, Mrs. Drew helped a lot. She teaches us."

"My wife will be most intrigued. I suppose in a few years you'll be one of our top designers? Paris and Rome, eh?"

She could not tell if he were laughing at her. He seemed genuinely interested and he never left off looking at her.

"Nothing startling like that," she said. "I shall try for a job in industry. I want something steady and well paid."

"I'm sure you'll succeed," he said. "By the way, Johnny's most remiss—he didn't mention your other name."

"Crockett," she said. "Iris Crockett."

He did not repeat it as Ascot had repeated Johnny's name, but there was the same queer, almost sickening, pause. He knew.

Then Johnny was back with their drinks and Caroline joined them.

"Why, Iris, how marvellous you and Johnny know each other already," she said. "He's my oldest friend, you know. I can tell you lots about him."

"What can you tell me about her?" Johnny asked. "I just can't see her at school."

"It isn't school—it's a technical college," Caroline said. "There's a big difference. Anyway, you can see all you want to know. She's a girl just like me."

"You are a mere chick," remarked Mr. Redmayne.

"Well, so's Iris when she has her hair down. You'll have to find out for yourself, Johnny. I'm not turning informer. Oh, she's got a brother in the Navy, though, and I must say I find that a bit intriguing. He's going to send her a sari from Singapore."

"Caroline, you made that up!" exclaimed Iris with a scarlet face.

"Well, the sari may be wishful thinking, but the brother's real."

"In the Royal Navy?" enquired Mr. Redmayne. Iris nodded. Somehow it never seemed to be so bad if you did not speak a lie.

"Let's dance," said Johnny suddenly.

When they were on the floor she said,

"I wish I'd known you were Johnny Redmayne from the first."

"Would it have made any difference?" he asked.

She thought the answer: "I wouldn't have fallen in love with you."

"Why?" he asked again.

She shook her head. She could never really wish that, no matter what was in store, for Johnny meant so much already that life would be empty without him.

"Wish something better than that," he persisted. "I'm going to see you get your wish. What do you wish for?"

"If I tell you I shan't get it." But she was wishing for Ma, for Tom, for herself.

"That's nonsense."

"I'd rather not."

"Are you all that superstitious? Come on."

"Well then, just that the way may be clear."

"That's a funny wish."

"It isn't really because until it is I can't wish anything for myself at all. You won't understand. People like you and Caroline can't be expected to understand."

"You mean because you come from

Sparrow's Yard—is that it? Because it belongs to Dad?"

"Partly. But that's not nearly all."

"But I love Sparrow's Yard," he said. "I love you for being there."

"But you can tell I don't belong in a house like this. Your father can see it. He won't be pleased if he sees you dancing with me too much. Johnny, I've got a hunch about this."

"Well, that's just too bad because I'm going to dance with you all I can and afterwards we're taking you home."

He spoke lightly but she knew he meant it and that it would be no use to insist on going by train. The Goldings would think it odd if she did.

When at last the party broke up Johnny linked her arm through his and they went out to the Rolls in which Mr. and Mrs. Redmayne were already sitting. Johnny's mother wore her mink coat over a slipper satin sheath of a magnolia shade. Iris had noticed it while they were having supper, priced the cut and quality and decided how much she could have made it for herself. As they drove off Mrs. Redmayne began to ask about her course at Abbeyfield.

"It all sounds so wonderful and clever," she said when Iris had satisfied her curiosity. "You young people of today don't realize how lucky you are."

Under cover of the rug across their knees Johnny took Iris's hand and held it. It was wonderful. Heavenly. She felt herself rising up on mounting peaks of excitement. Just this with the touch of a hand! With this she would be satisfied, she would never ask for more, she would not be able to bear any more. Nobody on earth could know more bliss than this.

As they neared home Mr. Redmayne asked for directions to Lantern Place.

"I'm afraid you can't drive up to it," she said. "Lantern Place is a kind of cul-de-sac and you reach it through an alley."

"Then you direct me as far as we can go and Johnny will see you the rest of the way."

Iris moved her feet uncomfortably under the rug. She did not want Mr. and Mrs. Redmayne to see where she lived. The approach was squalid. The narrow alley between the two overpowering old houses looked sinister in the dark and quite often courting couples found their way into it and flattened themselves against the walls as though they were trying to merge into the bricks. Old newspapers blew into the alley and got trapped there flapping from wall to wall and sometimes schoolboys took shelter with their screws of chips and dropped their greasy leavings on the ground.

"Is this the place?"

"Yes, but there's no need for anyone to come," Iris said. "Thank you very much for bringing me so far."

She was out of the car, but Johnny was out as well.

"It's a pleasure, Iris," Mr. Redmayne said.

"Good night, then, and thank you."

Mr. and Mrs. Redmayne were both smiling at her, but their eyes seemed to look past her as though they were trying to pierce the darkness of the alley and see what lay beyond.

She and Johnny did not speak till they reached her gate and then he said: "I wish I owned this little tucked-away corner. It would just suit me—it's out of this world."

"You haven't seen it by daylight yet," she said.

"I shan't change my opinion of it any more than I changed my opinion of you in that dress and with that hair. I saw through the disguise just like I did on Saturday when you were at the stall."

"I felt a fraud at Caroline's."

"You a fraud? You couldn't deceive anyone."

"Oh, Johnny, if you only knew," she said, thinking of Tom.

They were standing by the little low gate and the lamp light fell on the cockle shells that edged the minute flower beds. Her hand was in his and her face was turned up to him. He bent and brushed her cheek with his lips and then she was in his arms, clinging to him and turning her mouth to his. All her surging, pent-up emotions found release in that kiss. It was like nothing that had ever been before and it had to go on for ever and ever, this strange, wonderful ecstasy that they found in each other.

"When shall I see you again?" he asked. "I must see you tomorrow."

"I'm home all day," she said.

"Then I'll call about six. We can go to the sports club and dance."

Their lips met again and time was nothing until she heard a footstep and they tore apart vividly awake to their surroundings and to Cyril Redmayne, who stood quietly watching them.

"Your mother's waiting, Johnny," he said in an even tone.

Johnny's face was dark in the lamplight. He still had her hand in his but now he let it go, for his father was standing back so that he should precede him down the alley.

"Good night," Iris called softly.

Johnny's good night held a note of bravado. Mr. Redmayne said nothing. She listened till the sound of the Rolls died away, then she let herself into the house and crept quietly upstairs.

Her mother was fast asleep. She slipped out of her clothes as quickly as she could, unpinned the roses and put them in water, and then she slid between the sheets and curled up, but she felt cold with fear.

They had done nothing wrong: it would not have mattered if Gran or Aunt Camille had seen their kiss, but Mr. Redmayne was different. He had looked remorseless and there was something dead about him. She shivered. Perhaps he would find a way to prevent Johnny from coming again— this might have been their first and last kiss.

She buried her face in the pillow and began to think about him, desperately trying to recall everything that had happened, but soon the remembrance of the kiss reassured her and she lived through the ecstatic thrill of it until at last she fell asleep.

7

WHEN the Redmaynes reached home Cyril asked Johnny to put the car away and then he followed his wife into the house.

"Come in the dining room for a moment," he said. "I want to speak to you before Johnny comes in."

Helen Redmayne was already at the foot of the stairs and she turned to him with a puzzled look on her face.

"What's the matter?" she asked.

"Don't you realize who that girl was?" he asked, when he had closed the door behind her.

"Of course I do. You told me she's a Crockett from Sparrow's Yard," said Helen.

"Well, your son was kissing her good night and he took a long time about it," he said.

Helen's eyes opened wider, but she only remarked that she was not surprised. "She's so attractive. Beautiful, really. And

I'm sure I'd never have guessed her people keep a barrow from her accent," she said.

"She was putting that on, of course," he snapped.

"Well, I really don't know why you're so steamed up about it," she said. "There's not much wrong with a kiss."

"I won't have Johnny losing his head over that girl," said Cyril, his tone betraying his irritation. "I've hated that Sparrow's Yard crowd ever since I was a boy."

"I know, but that's a long time ago and those stalls are supposed to be one of the picturesque features of Villa Park," she replied.

"It's easy to say a thing's picturesque when it's on someone else's doorstep," complained Cyril. "I daresay I might have said the same if I'd never had to put up with them."

"They're only trying to make a living," said Helen tolerantly.

"Then they'd better make it while they can," he said. "Their days in the Yard are numbered."

"Cyril. You know what you promised your father," she said.

"I didn't promise. Father didn't ask me to," he said. "He told me he'd be happy if he knew they could go on trading there and I said I'd never stop them."

"And you won't, will you?"

"I shan't go back on my word, but if they move of their own accord don't put the blame on me," he answered.

"I was never any good at riddles," she said coldly, turning away from him.

"Listen, there's an old chestnut tree in that Yard and it's going to be pulled down tomorrow," he said.

"Whatever for?"

"Because it's in the way, but the Yard people aren't going to be pleased about it and I won't have Johnny involved with them. I'm going to warn him."

"If he's fallen for Iris your warnings won't make a scrap of difference."

"I'm not having any of that Sparrow's Yard crowd creeping in here and I want you to be quite clear about it," he said. "Young Johnny takes after my father and I don't want you encouraging any of his nonsensical ideas."

"All right," she said.

"It's been the dream of my life to turn

that place into something worth while and I won't be stopped now," he reminded her.

"Well, who's stopping you?" she asked. "For goodness' sake, Cyril!"

"You don't begin to understand," he said, and when she left him he wondered why she gave him so little sympathy.

Cyril Redmayne bore no resentment towards his mother because she had run away and left him alone with his outlandish father when he was a boy and as soon as it was possible he left home himself and went to join her. He was devoted to her and he often thought of the shock she must have had when Dr. Redmayne took her home after their honeymoon.

She had never seen his house till then, but when they drove into the Yard all the stallholders were waiting to greet them. She had never seen such a rabble in her life. There were women in shawls with their hair wound up in iron curlers and dirty children squalling and tumbling about all over the place.

"Is it some kind of market day?" she asked when they were indoors.

"Good heavens, no, my dear," Dr. Redmayne had said. "They come here every day and they are beginning to prosper at last. Don't you think that's splendid?"

"Do you mean that you allow them to make a market in our forecourt?" she demanded.

"Certainly. Look! There's Ascot Tagg over there. She used to sell from a basket when I first knew her but now she has her own stall. You'll love them all once you get to know them, Amanda."

She gazed despairingly round the dusty, half-furnished room he had taken her into. She could soon do something about that, but first those people would have to go. She repeatedly asked her husband to get rid of them, but he always refused, and so their marriage foundered before it began.

Cyril grew up to share his mother's feelings and when she went away he swore to rid the Yard of the traders one day. Then the day came. He was called to Dr. Redmayne's side when he was dying, and the sight of him propped up in his great bed in the huge, dingy room had moved him to compassion. The woman Ascot

Tagg was there and his father watched her with affection and grew worried if she left him. It would have been impossible to refuse his plea for the stallholders that day, but now he regretted it.

He felt tired and despondent and bitter. As he pulled himself out of the easy chair he had sunk into Johnny came in and put the car keys on the table. He had been such a long time that Cyril guessed he felt uncomfortable. Now was his chance to warn the boy and he plunged in and took it.

"Have you locked up?" he asked.

Johnny nodded and Cyril went on in an affable tone: "Not a bad party, was it? That Iris is quite an eye-catcher, but take my advice, old man, and steer clear. She's not our sort."

"Good Lord, she's terrific!" Johnny exclaimed. "I like her a lot. What have you got against her?"

"She's a Crockett. One of the Sparrow's Yard bunch and her family happens to be the worst of the lot. They're a crowd of liars, thieves and no-goods. You'll find life in Villa Park a lot pleasanter if you keep away from the Yard."

104

"I can't think why we never see things the same way," Johnny remarked. "I thought the Yard was wonderful when I went there just before Christmas. It's so full of life and colour. Honestly, Dad, I don't mind telling you it excited me. I only wish I could put it into music somehow."

"Don't forget the clank of chains, then," said Cyril, trying to keep the tone of spite out of his voice. "Iris Crockett's brother is serving four years for sticking up a wage van."

"Gosh!"

"I thought you'd be surprised."

"But how rotten for Iris and her mother!" exclaimed Johnny. "Honestly, Dad, you've got to hand it to her, haven't you?"

"Nonsense. The Crocketts are used to it —they're as bold as brass. People of their breed have got about as much feeling as crabs. And that Iris is a little liar, too. She told us her brother was in the Navy."

"You'd hardly expect her to say he's in prison," Johnny said. "And it was Caroline who told us, anyway. Sorry, Dad, but I still think she's the top."

"Well, don't go losing your head, then,"

Cyril said. "I want to see you having a good life, making the best of everything, getting the full value. Don't go and mess it up at the start."

Johnny did not reply immediately. Sometimes he felt almost sorry for his father and he knew it must have cost him a great deal to say so much. In return he could not be less than honest, but as he looked round their luxurious dining room he realized that he had always taken it for granted. He had never known anything but comfort. But what about Iris and the Crocketts? He thought of them in the cold of Sparrow's Yard, their hands hard and grimed, their feet frozen and their faces bitten by the wind.

His father was watching him with an anxious expression.

"Don't worry, Dad," he said. "I don't mean to mess up my life, but I do like Iris. She's not the kind of girl you meet every day."

"Perhaps not. Still, don't forget what I've told you. You've got good prospects at the bank and one of these days you'll be coming into everything I have. You don't want to make mistakes you'd regret."

"All right, Dad," Johnny said.

"Johnny," his father said, "don't see that girl again."

"I'm sorry, Dad. I can't promise that," Johnny said.

Cyril turned and threw the butt of his cigar into the fire. He wished wholeheartedly that he had not said so much because the look on his son's face confirmed his worst fears. Johnny really was interested in that girl.

"Very well. I expect I can trust your good sense," he remarked, trying to recapture the feeling of confidence which he thought he had established at the beginning of their conversation. Johnny met his eyes squarely.

"Good night, Dad," he said.

He went up to his room and crossed to the window. High above the moon was riding across the sky in the centre of a rainbow halo. He always thought of it now as a threatened moon and yet it looked serene enough. In some inexplicable way he now felt threatened himself and he knew he shared this feeling with Iris.

The conversation with his father had disturbed him deeply and now he could not have felt further removed from the boy who had bought some sprouts at a vegetable stall if there had been a world between them. He realized that there actually was a world between them, for the boy at the stall had never been in love. But he, Johnny Redmayne, was undoubtedly in love and it was the one thing he was absolutely sure of: he loved Iris Crockett and he was going to marry her one day.

He went to bed in a dream and woke up wondering what had happened and the whole of the next day was unlike any day he had ever spent and all because of Iris Crockett.

At the bank the chatter of his companions fell on his ear like sounds from another planet. He was in no doubt about his father's attitude to Iris, but it only made his own clearer, and as he thought over the situation his sympathy was with the people of Sparrow's Yard and would have been even if she had not existed.

Till now his life had been fairly simple and the only complication had been his music. Music! He never distinguished it by that name himself—it was just hurdy-gurdy, jingle, and yet Maurice Royal had seemed interested.

His mother always bore with him patiently, but his father showed signs of irritation because he spent so much time at the piano. Well, perhaps he wasn't any great shakes, yet the tunes came and he had to write them down. But now he had seen Sparrow's Yard he felt a new and compelling urge to create something different and he knew the time would come when he would have to gather the sound and the wonder of it together into a whole.

The day at the bank wore on and in the afternoon he was astonished to have a telephone call from Maurice Royal.

"Come and see me on Sunday week if you've nothing else to do," Maurice said. "Bring Iris if you'd like to."

If he would like to! "Thanks a lot," he said, "I'd love to."

He went back to his desk and tried to lose himself in his work, but it was impossible. He kept emerging from it feeling as bewildered as if he were waking from a dream and he knew it was because his life was no longer the carefree life of Johnny Redmayne. Now it was Johnny and Iris, and all the time he could feel his resolve strengthening almost in spite of himself. From the moment when he had stood at his window and seen the moon the night before till now, and so he faithfully believed till the last moment of his life, he would love Iris Crockett.

8

IRIS, too, was full of conflicting emotions the day after Caroline's party. When she thought of Johnny a wonderful new happiness filled her; then she remembered his father and she was afraid.

At breakfast Ma wanted to hear all about her evening, but knowing her feelings about the Redmaynes it was sometime before Iris had the courage to say that they had been at the Goldings'.

"Well, it's a pity you had to run into *them!*" she exclaimed when at last the news was out. "Still, I suppose it's not surprising seeing Mr. Golding's a lawyer and they've been neighbours. Same class of people, you see."

Iris stifled an expression of annoyance. Perhaps it was unconscious, but Ma had seized on yet another chance to emphasize an obstacle between herself and Johnny.

"The Goldings are very nice," she said defensively.

"And what about the Redmaynes?" enquired Melia. "Or didn't you get close enough to see?"

"Of course I did. She's quite pleasant and he's not bad in a way. The only thing is he's sort of"—she gave a little shiver—"frigid," she said.

"Yes, that's just about the right word for him," agreed Melia, and she sat gazing thoughtfully over her cup at the fire. She was worried about Iris. The girl had not been herself all over Christmas—half the time she was in the moon and it did not need much imagination to guess it was because she was thinking of Johnny. Johnny! Why did he have to be a Redmayne? He was tall and straight and fine, but it would be fatal if Iris were to lose her heart to him.

"I want the best for her," she thought fiercely, "but not Johnny. How could we ever mix with a family like his?"

Aloud she said: "I suppose you'll be going out with Alfie soon, then? I wish you'd gone out with him yesterday instead of to that party. He's a good boy. You ought to be a bit nicer to him."

"I know quite well what you're hinting

at," said Iris. "All right, I know Alfie's fond of me and he's good and honest and just our sort—but I could never think of him. Not now. Nor now I've met Johnny. Even if I were never to see Johnny again I shouldn't be able to think of anyone else."

"You know what I think about you and him being friends," Melia said after a pause. "And you don't even know him. How can you when you've only met him the twice?" she reasoned.

But she was puzzled because Iris was watching her with such a troubled expression and she suddenly realized it was because she was frightened and was longing to be reassured.

"What is it, my duck?" she asked gently. "What's upset you?"

"The Redmaynes brought me home last night and Johnny came right as far as the gate," Iris said. "He kissed me."

Melia gave a little deprecating cluck. If that was all why worry? He probably kissed every girl he took home, but she was pleased and touched to think Iris had confided in her.

"There's nothing in a good night kiss,

my ducky," she said. "Nothing for you to get upset about."

"But his father came up the alley and saw us and he made me feel terrible. It spoilt everything. He just stood there glaring."

"Oh!" exclaimed Melia. "That's different. I'm sorry that had to happen."

"He made me feel cheap. Did I imagine it or was he really angry?"

"Knowing him, I'd say he was angry. Still, it's no use fretting now. Christmas is over and there's no call for you to meet Johnny again. I don't suppose you will— you may be sure he knows what his father thinks of us now."

"He's going to take me to his sports club for a jive session tonight," Iris said. "He told me he'd call."

"You can take it from me he won't after this," said Melia.

"I'm sure he will," asserted Iris. "He'd never be like that."

Melia frowned. "It'll bring trouble, you and him getting so thick," she warned. "I wish you'd never met him. He'll make you discontented with home and then he'll go off with one of his own kind and leave you miserable."

"But he likes us all—he told me. He's not a bit like his father, truly he isn't. Wait till you know him, Ma. Oh, I wish you wouldn't look so worried!"

"I can't help being concerned about you," Melia said.

She had a dull ache in her heart and she set her mouth grimly as she thought of what Iris had told her. A first kiss and it had to end like that! But it hadn't been a mistletoe kiss, that was clear. It had been a real one. Still, it was a mean, wicked ending and it was typical of Cyril to have made Iris feel guilty.

After they had washed up and made the beds Melia went into Tom's room and opened the window.

"Smells damp in here. We'll have to give it a good airing," she remarked, and she went to the wardrobe and began to rearrange the clothes.

"Just look, this suit's all mildew marks!" she exclaimed. "There—and he's had no wear out of it."

"Never mind, it'll be old-fashioned now," said Iris.

Melia was at the window rubbing at the material in an effort to remove the marks. "We'll have to fit him out with all new I suppose," she said. "Roll on the day! He'll be all right when he comes home this time, Iris."

Her eyes went dreamy and her face became almost serene.

"We'll have the van all ready for him and that'll make his life worth living," she said, building her castles in the air aloud so that Iris might share them. "It's all right for old Wally to go to market with Dook and the cart, but you can't expect a young fellow like Tom to do the same. Might as well go back to the ark!"

Iris bit her lip. Ma was counting on Tom settling down to the life of a stall-holder, but he had never settled to anything yet and she wondered if he ever would. Meantime, while they waited for his release Melia worked as hard as two men put together, for she could never find trustworthy outside help.

"We want a man to help us now—it's too much for you," Iris said.

"Wally can still do a good day's work

and I can hump potatoes with the best of them," said Melia.

"You shouldn't have to," Iris asserted, and the sight of her mother's hard, thick hands holding Tom's jacket tore at her heart.

"Lucky I can drive," she thought. "Just let me pass that test and I can do a bit of good if Dook drops dead."

Next door Ascot and Wally had taken breakfast with Aunt Camille and when Iris went in afterwards they were eager to hear all about the party, too. She had to give them full details, including the news that the Redmaynes had been there, and this made Uncle Wally voluble.

"Stick to your own kind," he said. "There's nothing wrong with young Alfie."

"I never said there was, but he isn't Johnny," Iris answered, with a note of irritation in her voice.

"The boy may be all right, but that father of his is a mean-eyed kipper," Wally rumbled on. "Always was and always will be. We don't want to go getting mixed up with that crowd."

"You didn't mind being mixed up with

his grandfather," said Ascot. "Johnny's just like him, so he can count on me. The old doctor was a gentleman through and through."

"That's the danger," Wally said. "Stick to your own kind."

"Oh, stop it, Uncle Wally!" exclaimed Iris crossly. "I never did hear anyone carry on so. First Ma, now you. Just because he gave me a couple of roses and asked me to go dancing with him you talk as though we'd put up the banns."

Ascot grinned broadly, popped a lump of sugar in her mouth and sucked it noisily. "You've come quite a way in a few days, dearie," she said. "Don't forget the wish is father to the thought."

Iris blushed scarlet. Gran was right. It must have been in her mind or even deeper than that. Aunt Camille knitted a little faster, but she did not say anything, although she had a smile lurking at the corners of her mouth.

"I reckon I'm best out of here," Uncle Wally said in a huffy voice. "Better be on my way down to the Yard—see how Dook's getting on."

"Well, it's about time you took a stroll.

Dook'll be wondering where you've got to," Camille said.

"Don't notice your uncle, Iris," whispered Ascot. "He's crotchety. If he'd have got married and had some kids he'd have had more to occupy his mind."

Uncle Wally grunted as he tied his choker round his neck and then he stumped off down to the Yard, muttering to himself as he went.

It was a treat to be out of the house—there were too many women there. The open air was good and he had a busy day before him for he meant to scour out the shed. He reached the Yard just as a lorry turned in and he was surprised when it halted near the stable instead of driving up to the house.

Half a dozen men leapt out and began to unload ladders, ropes, saws, a jack and other tackle. At first he thought there was a mistake and that they had come to the wrong place, and he stood watching them uneasily, but by degrees he realized the purpose of their visit and he could not believe it. He did not know what to do, but when the men began to lever up the paving stones round the chestnut tree he ran over to them.

"'Ere!" he shouted huskily. "What do you think you're doing?"

"What do you think, mate?" enquired one of them affably.

"You can't cut down that tree," said Uncle Wally belligerently.

"Can't we? You watch us."

"That tree's been there hundred years or more. That's a Villa tree. You can't go cutting down that tree."

The man ignored him and Wally said: "I'll call the police, that's what I'll do. You can't come here mucking up this Yard. It ain't right."

A high-pitched whinnying from the stable seemed to add weight to his protest.

"There, hear that? Dook don't like it," Wally said. "You hear what he thinks? I'm going to the station to fetch the police."

"Is this your yard, guv?" asked one of the men, not unkindly.

"Can't say that, but I work here," replied Wally, taken aback but trying to sound confident. "Worked here all my life, I have. 'Ere! Leave that seat alone!

Where's people to sit if you take that seat away?"

"Have a fag?" The man opened a packet and offered it to Wally, who shook his head. He would not accept anything from an enemy and these people were all enemies.

"Look, we don't want to upset you," said the man, closing his packet reluctantly, "but we've got our orders and we've got to carry them out, see?"

Wally stuttered helplessly. He could think of nothing to say, but he felt so giddy that it seemed the ground rocked under his feet. He retreated to the stable and leaned against the wall with sweat on his forehead and an inward trembling that made him afraid to move. It would be useless to go to the police, he realized that, but he had a wild urge to rush home and fetch Ascot and Melia and to call out the Tilleys and the Cheeks and all the relations they could muster. When abuses like this happened people organized marches, they called meetings, signed petitions, drew attention to their wrongs. That was what the traders of the Yard should have done. Now they were too late.

He could hear the picks and shovels at work and he buried his face against Dook's strong, glossy neck. There were very few people in the High Road that day, for trade was slack and the stalls never reopened till the end of the week following Christmas. Wally thought bitterly that Cyril Redmayne had chosen his time well.

The sound of the choppers and saws mutilating the tree seemed to echo in his brain with a horrible intensity, yet somehow he could not bring himself to leave the scene. It held a dreadful fascination for him and after a while he left the stable and stood in the Yard watching. Presently he noticed someone with a camera and recognized him as Bill Ramsay from the local paper. Ramsay took several shots and he had a few words with the tree-fellers. Then he approached Wally.

"You'll be sorry about this," he remarked.

"It's like watching a human being hacked to pieces," Wally muttered. "Downright wicked. There won't be a green leaf in Villa Park time we're much older."

"Progress," said Ramsay.

"Progress be blowed!" burst out Wally angrily.

Ramsay murmured sympathetically. He had often taken pictures in the Yard and he knew the stallholders well. He usually got a good shot of Dook on Whit Mondays when he left the Yard to take part in the annual cart-horse parade in Regent's Park, and he had once won a competition with a picture of Ascot standing on an old backless kitchen chair waiting to take her place in the cart for the ride.

The crash of a falling branch interrupted Ramsay's recollections. Wally Tagg looked grey and shocked and the lines on his face seemed deeper than ever. He stared at the photographer blankly and suddenly the newspaper man saw a story.

Wally was too bemused to mind being photographed and he meekly led Dook out of the stable to be snapped beside the mutilated tree.

"I'm sorry about the tree," Ramsay said when he had finished. "People are going to miss it."

"Ah," said Wally, and he led Dook back to the stable and sat down to ruminate.

He was still there when the lorry rumbled out of the Yard at the end of the day. No good going home. Might as well let Melia and Ascot enjoy the rest of the evening in ignorance. He got out his clay pipe and lit it and then he remembered he had done nothing about cleaning out the shed. Tomorrow. He would do it tomorrow. But when he gazed across the bare Yard he wondered how he could find the heart tomorrow, or indeed if he would ever find the heart again.

9

AT about the time the tree-fellers were leaving the Yard Johnny Redmayne strode through the alley to Lantern Place and at the sound of his footsteps Iris felt her spirits rise and almost lift her off the ground.

"My word, doesn't he sound determined?" remarked Ascot. "He's got a lucky face, too."

"Have I?" asked Iris, as she went to the door.

Ascot looked at her seriously. "You've got a lovely face, my duck. I reckon in another two or three years it'll be a lucky face as well."

Iris did not wait for the knock. She opened the front door and Johnny stepped in and clasped her to him tightly. "I've been wondering if you were really true or if I'd dreamt you," he said, and the fears that had beset her that day melted away.

"I'm real—as real as you are," she said, and she led him into Aunt Camille's sitting room feeling relieved that Ma had decided to stay in their own house.

"Well, Johnny, and what sort of a day have you had?" enquired Ascot when they had exchanged greetings.

"A long one," he replied, with a glance at Iris.

"Then you'll be too tired to go dancing," teased Aunt Camille.

"Call the nasty contortions they do these days dancing?" snorted Ascot. "Why, if I wasn't so old I'd be shocked."

"Oh, go along with you. Iris does the twist beautifully," said Camille.

"So do I. I bet I could be the champion twister of Villa Park," said Johnny.

"Go on, then. Let's see you!"

"I'd shake the house down and I'd hate to do that," he said. "I've fallen for Lantern Place." He stirred the tea Aunt Camille poured for him and sipped it appreciatively. "It's all gorgeous and homey—like the smell of cakes baking," he said.

"Yes, that's my caraway seed and it's just out of the oven," remarked Camille. "Would you like a piece with some fresh butter? It takes a bit of beating."

"Would I?" said Johnny ecstatically.

Iris was putting on her coat. It was so wonderful to see Johnny sitting there drinking tea and waiting for Aunt Camille to cut the cake just as though he belonged. It gave her a marvellous feeling of safety. But she would have to tell him about Tom; she had made up her mind about that.

She waited to do so till they emerged from the alley and then she stopped and said, "Johnny, there's something I must tell you before we go any further."

They were under the lamp and her face was white by its light.

"It's a secret—something we never talk about outside the family—not unless we have to."

"Iris, you're speaking to me as though I'm a stranger," he said.

"It's not an easy thing to have to say. It's about my brother. I said he was in the Navy when we were at Caroline's. Well, he's not. He's in prison," she said harshly.

She had withdrawn her hands from his because she knew she would not be able to bear it if he were to withdraw his when he heard. Now he groped for them and held them tightly.

127

"He got four years. It was a wage hold-up and there was a whole crowd of them in it. Tom's been in trouble since he was a boy and sometimes I think he'll never be out of it."

"It's grand of you to trust me," Johnny said. "It must have made life pretty grim for you—all this."

"Oh, if you knew the half of it!" she cried. "Sometimes when I'm in class I'll notice the sun shining on a tree outside and then I'll think 'Tom's out on exercise now,' and it's just as though I can see him trying to get where he'll feel the sun on his face."

"And all this is going through your mind when you're trying to concentrate?"

"I don't seem able to stop it. Sometimes the lecturer stops and says, 'Iris Crockett have I your attention?' and then everyone sniggers and says, 'Poor old Iris, she has got it badly.'"

"And then what do you do?"

"Oh, I go red in the face and get in an awful temper and I just long to shout out, 'So would you have it badly if your brother was walking round a prison yard in someone else's smelly old shoes.' So now you know, Johnny. That's what I'm like."

"You didn't think this would make any difference to the way I feel about you, did you?" he asked. "Nothing's ever going to alter that, Iris. Let's get that straight from the start."

"I couldn't help being scared."

"Don't ever be again."

She took a deep, shuddering breath like a sob. "If only we can be together," she said, and her voice was tight with one of the sudden fears that came to her even at moments of highest happiness. It was an inexpressible, terrible fear and it came whenever she thought of the future. It came when other girls talked of their hopes and ambitions and were gay and light-hearted, for her own hopes were subject to her loyalty to Ma and that was born of something deeper than love and the bond of relationship.

It came from a sense of justice. Rough justice, perhaps. Ma had suffered because of Dad and because of Tom, so she had to see that Ma didn't suffer any more. She had to see that Ma kept going until Tom was free. People of their own sort, people of the Yard, understood and accepted the restrictions these responsibilities imposed but would Johnny be able to? It was asking a great deal and she knew it.

His arms were round her, strong and reassuring.

"We will be together," he said. "Don't you worry about that. We're going to be."

"You really mean it?"

"Listen," he said. "I love you."

She looked up at him, incredulous. "But that's how I feel about you," she said. "Oh, how I wish we could stay here all night, Johnny, just like this! I've never been so happy."

The foggy air, the street lamp, the dingy street, were beautiful. She did not even know she was cold until he told her so.

"You're frozen," he said. "Come on, let's get moving. What did you want to stop under that lamp-post for?"

"It's a lovely, heavenly, darling lamp-post," she said. "I could float up to the top and balance there!"

"Let's float along to the bus stop instead," he said.

Iris was thrilled by her evening at the sports club; the band was good and the crowd lively and Johnny's colleagues looked interested when he introduced her.

"Lucky old Redmayne," they said.

"I know I am," said Johnny, and he and Iris danced till they were both exhausted. They could have gone on till morning, but they left in time to catch the last prosaic bus which somehow became enchanted when they entered it.

They strolled along Villa Park High Road with arms entwined and then they came to Sparrow's Yard and saw the chestnut tree. It's trunk, shorn of branches, lay across the Yard and there was a gaping hole where the roots had been. The sight of it was even more horrifying than the notice board had been and Iris stood still, frozen.

"Why, what a rotten idea!" Johnny exclaimed. "What on earth have they cut it down for?"

"To clear the way for the building," she said, in a voice that shook.

Then she touched his arm. "Look— there's Uncle Wally," she whispered.

The old man was just leaving the stable and they watched him close the doors. He stood leaning against the door for a moment with his head on his arms and then he came towards them, but he came slowly, dragging his feet and he did not notice them till she spoke.

"Why, Iris, what are doing here?" he asked, and she noticed how grey his face looked in the cold light.

"We're just on our way home," she said. "You don't look well, Uncle Wally."

"I don't feel it, neither. You wouldn't feel well if you'd stood by and seen that tree cut down. What's Dook going to say when summer comes and there's not a bit of shade? Nice thing. You can see what'll happen to Villa Park if they give people like Redmayne a free hand."

"Oh, do hush, Uncle. Don't you see Johnny's here?" Iris said.

"Why should I hush because of him? You come on with me, my girl," said Uncle Wally, giving Johnny an unfriendly look. "There's no call for you to come any further, young man," he said.

"I'm awfully sorry about this, Mr. Tagg," said Johnny. "I really am. I'd no idea it was going to happen."

"Oh, please don't let's have an argument!" Iris cried. "Johnny can't help it."

132

"It's a pity you Redmaynes came here," said Uncle Wally fiercely. "Got no respec', you haven't. If you know what's good for you you'll go on home and keep out of Iris's way in future. She don't want none of you. You coming, Iris?"

She hesitated. In front of her stood poor old Uncle Wally and the sight of him filled her with pity, while at her side was tall, strong young Johnny. She had to choose, but it almost broke her heart.

"I'll be along presently, Uncle, but Johnny's bringing me home," she said firmly.

Uncle Wally stared as though he did not believe her. Then he straightened his hat, squared his shoulders and turned away. They watched him go and when he was out of earshot Iris said: "I hurt him, Johnny. It's terrible."

"I know. But we can't let a thing like this come between us," he said.

"It's going to be hard to stop it. Your father didn't like me, did he? There's no need to deny it. I could feel it too strongly."

"He doesn't know you," Johnny said.

"He doesn't need to. He has always

hated the Yard people and I'm one of them."

"I love you. Isn't that enough?"

"He'll separate us."

"Not unless we're weak. We've got to be strong."

"He's powerful," she said.

"So are we if we stand together," Johnny said. "That's what we're going to do."

And he kissed her cold lips in the starlight and drew her arm through his and they turned towards Lantern Place.

10

THE encounter with Johnny and Iris did Uncle Wally good, for it released some of his pent-up emotions. He reached home to find Melia waiting on Camille's doorstep.

"Wherever have you been, Uncle Wally?" she asked. "We were just going to send out a search party."

"Did you know young Iris is out with that Redmayne?" he challenged.

"Of course I did."

"Then you're a fool to let her go." He pushed his dirty old trilby to the back of his head and followed her into the sitting room.

"Our girl arm in arm with that stuck-up young toad! I'd kick him over the Villa if I only had the strength."

"Oh, come on, Wally!" exclaimed Ascot. "Time you got a girl and found out what it's all about! How about Glad Cheek? She's always had her eye on you."

"Then she can take it off," said Wally.

"This isn't the time to turn waggish, Ascot, I can tell you that. We're in trouble."

Ascot heaved herself to the edge of her chair and asked anxiously, "Nothing wrong with Dook, is there?"

"Dook's all right. Least, he's as right as he can be seeing as our chestnut tree's been cut down," rasped Wally.

"Cut down?" echoed Ascot. "Whatever for?"

"How should I know?" returned Wally angrily. "All I know is they've cut it down. Got their orders, they told me."

"Who from?" demanded Melia.

"That Cyril Redmayne, of course," said Wally. "Who else?"

The lines on Melia's forehead deepened and she began to rock herself backwards and forwards in her chair. So many people had smiled knowingly when she had told them the stalls were to be allowed to stay in the Yard.

"Well, we can't afford to fall out with Mr. Redmayne. It's his tree and if he cuts it down we must just lump it," said Ascot.

Melia drew in a long, shuddering breath because she could not bear to think of the

Yard without the tree. It was not an unmixed blessing, what with the falling leaves all slippery in autumn, and yet they loved it. The branches spread out and made a great tent and a summer shower would bring crowds to shelter under it. In late spring it was smothered with clusters of white flowers and she remembered pulling off the blossoms when she was a child and biting the ends to taste the sweetness that attracted the bees.

The tree was a landmark. Without it the whole character of the Yard would alter and she shivered at the thought.

"I wish the Redmaynes were at the bottom of the sea, lock stock and barrel," she said.

"We'd have been out on the street corners with a miserable basket of lemons as likely as not if it hadn't been for Dr. Redmayne—just you remember that, Melia," said Ascot. "We've done well in our time."

"We've got to keep on doing well. There's Tom to think of," Melia answered.

"He's not likely to be forgotten," said Ascot. "But don't let's start falling out with the Redmaynes. That Cyril may be hard but Johnny's all right. I put my money on him."

"So do I," echoed Camille. "And he's struck with Iris. Anyone can see that."

"Time all that nonsense was put a stop to," said Wally. "I just seen them both down by the Yard and I told him what I thought about his dad."

"Then you shouldn't have," said Camille.

"Young Iris wants a good hiding. Wouldn't come home with me when I asked her—preferred to be with him. Going against her own kind, she is. And what use is a fellow like that to her? He'll waste her time and give her nothing but big ideas."

"So long as he doesn't give her a big stomach I reckon she can sort out the ideas for herself, Wally Tagg," said Ascot.

"My Iris would be an asset to any man, Redmayne or not," shouted Melia, thumping the table. "She's as good as she looks, I'd have you know."

"All right. Don't go for me," lamented Wally. "I never said as she wasn't. It was Ascot came out with that rude remark."

"Just look at us! All falling out with one another because Mr. Redmayne's cut down a tree!" exclaimed Camille. "For goodness' sake don't let's go looking for trouble or we'll find it, sure as fate."

But they continued to talk round the subject and although not one of them put their overriding fear into words it cast its shadow on them and filled their silences with forebodings. Sparrow's Yard belonged to Cyril Redmayne now and they all knew he had it in his power to rob them of their livelihood.

At last Melia said: "Camel's right. There's no sense meeting trouble halfway."

"That's sense and the best thing we can do is sleep on it," agreed Ascot.

Camille sat on by the fire when the others had gone. Soon Harry would be home. They were all right, she and Harry; they managed well and they were happy but then they were so lucky. She had enjoyed so much richness—the places she had been and the people she had known! Even now she had only to stretch out her hands to have further pleasures and delights put into them. If Harry ever got out of work or if the rigours of winter tried her too severely there was always Maurice's offer of a place in the sun. He had a house in Provence to which he invited them every year. They had never yet been.

"There's only one thing wrong with it," Maurice always said. "I've got a lovely cook, but the place needs you and Harry to look after it. How about it, eh?"

The offer was renewed at frequent intervals and sometimes the idea of it filled her with the longing to get away. She was so deep in her thoughts that she did not hear Iris come in till she was beside her, kneeling on the rug and holding out her hands to the fire.

"What were you thinking about, Auntie?" she asked.

"Matter of fact I was just thinking how lovely it must be at Maurice's farm. Poor old Maurice!"

"He's rich. He's got everything."

Camille shook her head. "Everything but his wife, Iris. He never got over losing her and the baby. She was a lovely girl, was Millie, with such a pretty voice, and we were all young together, going round the halls. You may be sure he'd give up all his success to have just one of those days again."

"If anything awful like that happened to me I should just die," said Iris. "Even now, Auntie Camille, if I were to lose Johnny I think I should die."

"Oh no, you wouldn't," said Aunt Camille. "You've got Ma to think of. Besides, it's selfish to die—even inside yourself."

Without warning the tears began to spill down Iris's face. "We had such a wonderful evening till we got to the Yard," she sobbed. "I love Johnny and he loves me, but whatever happens I won't leave Ma, Auntie. Not till everything's all right for her."

"There, there, ducky," Camille said. "Everything will be right in time. You're young. There's lots of time for you and Johnny."

But as she soothed Iris she could not help thinking of Melia and wondering what lay ahead for her. She had had so little happiness in her life, though no one could blame her for marrying that Quick Crockett when she had the chance. He was a villain with his blue eyes and sunburned face and he stole Melia's senses. No wonder. You only had to hear his voice to be cheered up when you were low. He was a tonic and that was the trouble. Everybody wanted him. No woman could hold Quick for long, but he did come back to Melia. Still, by that time the damage was done and Tom was out of hand.

"There now, you go on home to Ma now, Iris," Aunt Camille said, when she saw the girl was calmer. "Try to keep her from worrying about the Yard. That's the best way."

Iris had not been gone long when Camille heard Harry's key in the door. Suddenly she felt young, alert and even pretty and her weariness fell from her shoulders at the sight of him. She flung her arms round his neck and rubbed her cheek against his face.

"My word, it's good to be home," he said.

"Come in by the fire," she said. "Did you have to walk?"

"No, the bus was waiting."

"Full house?"

"Solid. Can't see it ever closing," he said.

She spooned sugar into the tea she had made him and stirred it, and she watched him lovingly as he took his first long, loud sip.

"Ah, there's no one makes tea like you do, Camel," he said.

She was smiling to herself because his praise never failed to warm her heart, and she began to sing softly. Her Harry was not handsome, he was short and rather seedy-looking and he defeated all her efforts to smarten him up. He had a drooping, tobacco-coloured moustache and his nose took on a pinkish hue in the cold weather, but she loved him and was never happier than when they were together.

When she took in his supper she was still singing.

"What's the tune?" he asked, as he began to eat. "Something out of a new show?"

"No, it's Johnny Redmayne's song," she said. "Like it?"

"Um. Quite a good little tune," he said. "Had a good day, Camel?"

"Well, I don't know," she said. "Good

143

in parts, I suppose. One thing's certain, though. Iris has fallen for Johnny and if I'm not much mistaken he's fallen for her. In fact I'd say they're cut out for each other."

"Oh," said Harry, wiping his chin, "that'll cause a flutter in the Redmayne camp. It wouldn't surprise me if they get their bows and arrows out."

"I hope not for Melia's sake," said Camille anxiously. "Still," she went on, "things never turn out the way you expect so it's no use worrying."

And with that she began to clear the table, but she did not sing any more.

11

THE old year went out mournfully for the stallholders now that changes in the Yard were actually taking place and when they heralded in the new at the Duke's Head Mrs. Tilley advised everyone to look on the dark side.

"Then you won't be disappointed," she said. "The Redmayne block will ruin us for sure. I lay that Cyril's got plans for the Yard that'd make our hair stand on end if we only knew."

"Where does he keep them, then?" demanded Ascot. "Harry's been to the Town Hall and there's nothing there to fright you."

"Ah, but there's more under his hat than you're likely to guess," returned Mrs. Tilley heavily. "He don't put everything on paper."

Princess Potter disagreed. "He's building well back and there'll still be plenty of room for us," she argued.

"Wishful thinking," sniffed Mrs. Tilley. "We'll all be out by midsummer."

"Oh, stuff and nonsense," declared Ascot loudly. "Stick a feather in your hat, Tilley, why don't you? Gawd, it's enough to make a woman paint her nose red!"

"All right, you may laugh," said Mrs. Tilley gloomily.

"Well, who's side are you on?" asked Ascot. "I say we're all going to come up smiling, you as well."

Melia did not share Ascot's faith but she echoed her words, as did Winnie and Glad Cheek, but Mrs. Tilley's face looked as glum as a block of lard when she drained her glass at closing time.

"We shall see," she said. "Happy New Year, all."

Ernie Tilley never said a word all through. He drummed on the table top with his thick, pale fingers and blinked his poor, pale eyes. Mrs. Tilley and Alfie had wheeled him to the pub and he sat there in his invalid chair at the head of the table looking vaguely from one to the other and they all smiled and nodded at him and did their best to encourage him.

There was no doubt Mrs. Tilley had her

plateful, Melia thought, but she didn't have to be quite so glum. Far better to look cheerful like Ascot and Princess Potter. Mrs. Tilley's gloom was enough to attract ill fortune.

Melia had decided that it would be wiser not to mention their acquaintance with Johnny Redmayne to the others, for she still expected it to be short-lived in spite of Camille's contrary opinion. He came to Lantern Place every evening and there was no doubt he enjoyed himself there in spite of Uncle Wally's unconcealed hostility. Most likely he was at Camille's now and she guessed they would be having a sing-song and a laugh over the albums of photographs.

It even appeared that Maurice had invited Johnny to his flat and he and Iris were going there on Sunday week. She was anxious about Iris and she was afraid of Cyril Redmayne. In time Johnny would come to realize the disadvantages of a connection with a family like theirs and then Iris would suffer.

She glanced at Alfie, who was wiping his mouth with the back of his hand. He was good and steady and reliable, but what chance did he stand with Iris now that she knew Johnny? As the bells rang out she wondered what lay before them in the year ahead and she prayed that they might still be trading peacefully in Sparrow's Yard when it ended.

During the first week of the New Year the demolition men moved in on the old house and a smell of burning wood from Dr. Redmayne's garden wafted over the stalls. Occasionally a burst of flame could be seen through the hedge for the trees round the house were being felled and burnt as well.

Iris had not worked at the stall since Christmas and on her first Saturday there she found the Yard bare and strange without the tree.

"You'll soon get used to it," Ascot said. "'Sides, don't tell me you've nothing in your head but the Yard these days."

Iris was almost ashamed to admit how true this was, for Johnny filled her mind almost exclusively and she knew the peculiar sensation of living on two planes. She served vegetables automatically while she imagined herself alone with him amid scenes of unmitigated bliss.

Sometimes a chance remark dragged her back to reality. She heard a woman calling her little boy: "Tom, come here, will you?" and the name stirred her and gave her a guilty feeling as though she were enjoying a forbidden pleasure. Then Glad Cheek came over to buy some root vegetables and said: "Your Ma looks worried, duck. Poor dear, she's aged this last year and no mistake."

Mrs. Tilley said heavily: "To think we should live to see the chestnut go, Iris. What next, I wonder?" and she sent Alfie over with cocoa for Ma more than once that morning and whenever Iris looked over at their stall she could see Mrs. Tilley's large square face set in an expression of gloom under a heavy black velour hat.

Mrs. Tilley's hat was trimmed with black sequins and it had hitherto been her Sunday one. Now as an everyday hat it seemed to detract colour from the fruit on her stall and to infect her side of the Yard with a funereal atmosphere.

Then, just before lunch, Johnny came and when he strode across the Yard, conspicuous in the jostling crowd of

Saturday shoppers, Iris felt her heart give a leap because it was the first time he had been there since that first enchanted Saturday.

Melia saw him crossing the Yard too and she remembered how she had felt long ago when Quick Crockett came to the stall and stole her heart away. She touched Iris's arm and said unexpectedly: "Here he is, Iris. You'd better take the afternoon off and show him round the Villa."

"Why, what a terrific idea!" exclaimed Iris. Then she hesitated and added: "How will you manage without me, though?"

"Gracious me, I've done it before, haven't I? Take my tip, though. Don't talk to him about the way things are going here."

Johnny, who had not heard this exchange, joined them as she finished speaking and Melia said: "Iris is off duty, Johnny, so take her out somewhere. Look out now, there's Florrie Perks in the offing."

Iris did not have to be told again and as she and Johnny left the stall they heard the blatant voice of Florrie Perks exclaiming over the chestnut tree.

"'Cor, if that dirty old tree hasn't gone at last," she shouted. "Dirty old leaves and all. Nice to see the place cleaned up a bit. We've only got the scum left now!"

"Whoever is she?" Johnny asked.

"The one Dad went off with. I told you," Iris said. "That's her son with her."

"He looks quite decent," Johnny said.

"He's ever so like Tom," she admitted. "He's a proper Crockett."

Florrie was in one of her worst moods. "Yah, you'll all be swept up like a lot of dirty leaves," she bellowed. "We'll have nice clean motor cars here instead of you dirty old lot. Look at old Ma Tilley! She'll look pretty sitting in a dustbin, won't she?"

"Do come on, Johnny," Iris urged, for Florrie was crossing the Yard now and she was liable to stop by their stall and tell anyone who cared to listen the story of her life.

Johnny left the Yard reluctantly and they walked along the High Road, but they had not gone far when they heard someone calling and they turned to see Raymond Perks pursuing them.

"What is it?" Iris asked coldly as he caught them up.

"Just I'm sorry about this and the other day at the station, too," he said. "Mum's not herself these days."

"Well, it's not your fault. I shouldn't let it worry you," said Iris. "It's like water on a duck's back to me."

As she turned to catch up with Johnny who had gone on a few paces Raymond said shyly, "Well, happy New Year, Iris."

"Oh, thanks," she answered in a far softer tone. "The same to you."

Their eyes met for a moment and then Raymond turned back to the Yard.

"What do you think of that?" Iris said, as she fell into step with Johnny again. "That's the first time we've ever spoken."

"It was pretty decent of him," Johnny remarked. "His mother must be quite a handful. Still, her life can't have been particularly easy."

"She hasn't anyone but herself to blame."

"That goes for all of us," he said.

"I suppose it's easy for you to feel compassionate," Iris said, "but I don't think I ever shall."

"You can't see her straight and no one could expect you to," he said. "But to me she's a bit tragic—for one thing she looks almost burnt out. You know, I keep thinking of Sparrow's Yard as music and Florrie Perks is a magnificent, discordant note—she's a kind of wonderful clamour. In fact the whole place is like that. I can hear it."

"For me it's mostly colour—oh, and smells, too. Bonfire smoke and chrysan-themums. But I want to hear the music you make of it. It must be wonderful to feel it that way."

"But I've so much to learn," he said. "Sometimes I think I shall be ninety before I know the first thing."

They had turned into Lantern Place and a delicious, savoury smell greeted them.

"Ooh," he said, standing still and sniffing. "Iris, you do have scrummy food!"

"That's Gran's cooking," she said, and she pushed Ascot's door open and led him through to the kitchen where her grand-mother was standing at the stove.

"Who smelt my Poor Man's Goose, eh?" Ascot asked.

"We did and Johnny's dying to taste it, so I hope you've got plenty," Iris said.

"Of course I have, my love," replied Ascot. "Camel's gone out, so I made it for a treat. Come along, both of you. Sit you down."

The kitchen table was already laid with a spotless coarse white cloth and Ascot opened the oven and produced a large pie dish in which she had baked a concoction of liver, onion and pig's fry seasoned with sage and topped with a thick crust of potato.

"I once made this dish for your grandfather," she told Johnny as she piled his plate high. "He always asked for it again."

"No wonder. We never had anything half so tasty at home," he said.

"Had a busy morning?" enquired Ascot. "Anything going on down at the Yard?"

"Florrie Perks turned up and started to shout and what do you think? Raymond ran after us and said he was sorry about it. He even wished me a happy New Year."

"Did he? The poor little varmint," Ascot said. "Remember how him and his sister used to beg for a ride on Dook when they were little? Used to run into the Yard

154

all eager and hopeful, but old Wally only ever growled at them."

She smiled softly at the recollection of the two children with their large, questioning eyes and the taciturn, embarrassed Wally.

"Get along out of it," he would growl.

"Beaver! Get your face shaved! Mum's got a razor—want to borrow it?" The children would draw their fingers across their throats and make horrible choking noises before they ran away, whooping and unvanquished.

"Not their fault," Ascot used to say, and she would give them a few apples when no one was by.

"Johnny and I are going round the Villa this afternoon," Iris was saying. "Gran! You're not listening."

"I was thinking of that Raymond—and of Florrie," Ascot said.

"What do you want to think of them for?"

"You mentioned them, my duck. And I heard something bad about her today. She's to have an operation—going into Abbeyfield hospital soon."

Iris was silent for a moment. For the

first time in her life she was trying to put herself in Raymond's place and it occurred to her that Florrie must have been coming from hospital when she and Aunt Camille had encountered her at the station before Christmas.

"You'd better go and get changed while I make a cup of tea," Ascot said, interrupting her thoughts. "I daresay you can do with one, eh?"

"Yes please," Iris said.

After she had gone Ascot pushed the dish over to Johnny and said: "Go on— scrape it out. Your grandfather always did —said that was the best part of the meal."

He did not need to be told twice. He liked Ascot immensely and felt at home with her and as she pottered about the kitchen she talked of Florrie Perks.

"She was a handsome girl—shame she had to put her eye on Quick. She upset my poor Melia properly," Ascot said. "Still, it's no good bearing resentment— that's what I say."

"I agree with you, Mrs. Tagg," Johnny said.

"Mrs. Tagg? Who's that? I'm Ascot— that's what everyone calls me and you must do the same. Born Ascot week, I was. That's how I got my name. I called Camel after a nice little mare that won the Oaks and Melia, Amelia Arethusa that is, she was called after a very nice little horse Wally used to know. With Dook it was the other way round. Wally called him after a man—the Dook of Villa Park. You'll see his picture at the Villa."

She rambled on and Johnny listened attentively, for he could not hear too much about the people who surrounded Iris. He knew without any doubt that he loved her dearly and as soon as it was possible he meant to marry her if she agreed. It would mean waiting, for he knew she would not leave home for some time and he had to improve his own position. There would be no help from his father.

Deep down he knew his father's animosity towards the Crocketts would be almost impossible to root out and he felt glad he was of age. He was certain his father would never consent to their marriage.

Iris came in at that moment, looking so beautiful with her fair, shoulder-length hair and wonderful dark eyes that he could not say anything when he saw her. She smiled at him and took the tea Ascot handed her, and when she had finished it she went round and hugged her grandmother.

"You are a duck, Gran," she said.

"Here, lay off!" cried Ascot. "I'm drinking my tea. Go on out with you while the sun still shines."

"Thanks for the lunch, Ascot," Johnny said. "It was absolutely super. I can see why my grandfather fell for you."

"It wasn't only the cooking," she said. "Still, come again, Johnny. Any time."

It was a perfect afternoon for the park because the trees made a Chinese picture against the sky. Johnny and Iris walked by the lake and every now and then they stopped to wonder at the brilliance of a duck, and they exclaimed at the almost unbelievable perfection of the mandarins with their smooth feathers arranged in designs that made them look like little painted toys.

Neither of them had ever been in a place that was so exquisite in the company of the one with whom they had just fallen in love and this state of being lent a radiance to everything they saw.

Johnny said the Villa was a fairy palace conjured out of the air and they went inside and wandered through the rooms and they marvelled at the painted ceilings and exclaimed at the views from the windows. Eventually they sat on a seat beneath the dome roof of the central hall.

"Isn't it quiet? I don't believe there's anyone here but us," said Iris.

"It doesn't sound like it," Johnny said, and he put his arm round her.

Occasionally an odd visitor, wandering through the rooms, noticed them on the bench and tiptoed past with only a quick glance in their direction, for they were lost to the world. But one couple on a sight-seeing tour was more interested in Iris and Johnny than they were in the Villa.

Cyril Redmayne had brought his wife there that afternoon and they were on their way out when they realized who the young people were and saw that they were completely unaware of everything but each other.

"Come away, Cyril," whispered Helen, as he stopped in the doorway. "You're not going to speak to them, are you? Oh, you are mean!"

Cyril had advanced into the hall and planted himself in front of them before she finished speaking.

"Well, this is a surprise," he said. "I'd no idea you were interested in historical buildings, Johnny."

Johnny looked up startled. "It's a surprise to see you here too, Dad. As a matter of fact Iris has been showing me round. She's quite an authority on the Villa."

"That is nice," put in Helen before Cyril had a chance to say anything cutting. "I'm interested in old houses, too, and this one is really lovely. It's all quite new to me, but I expect it's just a part of your life, isn't it, Iris?"

"I've been coming here ever since I could walk," said Iris gratefully. "Uncle Wally used to bring me. We used to meet a young man walking in here who always talked to Uncle Wally about horses and then a lot later on we found out he was the Duke."

"Really? How interesting," Helen said. She would have liked to say more but her

160

husband's presence prevented her. She knew he was furious because Johnny was with Iris but she could see nothing wrong with this pretty, pleasant girl.

"I think we've seen everything, my dear," Cyril said. "Can we give you a lift anywhere, Iris?"

"Thank you, but I like to walk," she said.

"You'll be home to dinner then, Johnny," said Cyril in a tone of command.

"No, I'm taking Iris out this evening," Johnny replied.

There was a pause and then Cyril said, "I see," and Helen tried to compensate for his coldness by saying she hoped they would have a lovely evening, but her affability only underlined her husband's manner.

As soon as they were alone they both drew in a deep breath and Iris suggested they should go, too. Some of the magic had gone out of the afternoon.

"I'm sorry we met them," Johnny said. "They've spoilt it."

"Your father certainly tried to. There's no doubt about it—he hated seeing you with me. You can't deny it, Johnny."

"Oh, he's just got a bee in his bonnet about Sparrow's Yard," Johnny said.

"You're right, and that's what worries me," she said.

They were standing at a point where six broad avenues met.

It was a vantage point which only someone like Iris, who knew the park really well, could find. It gave anyone who stood there the feeling of being far, far away from the outside world, for the paths themselves seemed endless, each stretching away towards some piece of statuary which the various dukes of Villa Park had brought home from their travels.

"It doesn't matter which path we take," she said in a flat little voice, because she had been seized by a terrible fear that she was going to lose him. Already he seemed remote, unfamiliar. There was no smile on his face.

"But there is only one path for us," he replied. "I love you and I want to marry you. Do you feel the same about me?"

Her fear dissolved in a flood of pure joy as she recognized his strength and determination.

"Oh yes!" she cried. "Yes, I do."

"Then we can look forward," he said. "We can make plans for the future."

"But I don't see how we can—there's no hope for years," she said. "For me the idea of marrying is like a lovely bubble, all wonderful colours, that floats just out of reach and bursts when you touch it."

"But why?" he asked.

"Because of everything. Ma, Tom, the Yard. I'm tied to them. I'm in prison, Johnny."

"Then so am I," he said. "We're never really free agents, no matter how we may kid ourselves. But if Ma needs your help I shall be there as well, Iris. We'll get married as soon as we can but from now on we're in this together. We're just—well —we're just a pair."

"Oh dear, you are funny," she said. "And wonderful. Johnny, I do love you!"

"Me too. Come on—let's run," he said, and he took her hand and started to race her along the path that led to the gate.

"I can't keep up," she gasped.

"Oh yes, you can. Are you going to tell your people about us?"

"I shall keep it to myself till we get back from Maurice tomorrow night. I daren't think of what Ma will say. She'll be terrified of what your father will do."

"My father has got us to contend with —you and me. I told you that before," he said.

"Can't run any more," she said, dragging behind him now.

He stopped, flung his arms round her and hugged her to him.

"At any rate you're not cold any more," he said, and in the gathering dusk he saw that her cheeks were glowing and her eyes sparkled. She looked as though she hadn't a care in the world.

"That's how she's always going to look when we're married," he thought, and he took her arm soberly and they walked through the gates trying to give the impression that they were a staid married couple and not succeeding at all.

12

WHILE Iris and Johnny sat in the blissful gloom of a coffee bar that evening the traders of Sparrow's Yard were holding a council of war in the Duke's Head. With every day that passed they felt less sure of their future and now Winnie and Glad Cheek shared Mrs. Tilley's gloom.

"We ought to ask Mr. Redmayne straight out," declared Alfie Tilley. "Let's make a deputation."

"No harm in that," said Winnie Cheek. "Know where we stand then, and we can act according."

"That's all very well, but he's not an easy man," put in Melia. "Who's going to speak to him?"

"Let's get there and see how the cards fall," Mrs. Tilley said. "Maybe Alfie could ask him."

"It ought to be someone older than me," objected Alfie. "And it's got to be someone who's working there, like Wally or you, Mum."

"Not me," said Mrs. Tilley firmly. "I'd lose me tongue the minute I saw him. You, Melia. How about you?"

"Lor', no!" exclaimed Melia in horror. "Not me, for goodness' sake."

"Well, you want to stay there, don't you?" asked Mrs. Tilley. "You got twice the nerve I have."

"Go on, Melia," urged Princess Potter. "You'd do it fine."

The suggestion appalled Melia. She dreaded the idea of meeting Cyril Redmayne and the fact that Johnny was seeing Iris regularly made her still less willing. But the other stallholders were in ignorance of this affair, so she could not excuse herself on that score. They all knew that Alfie was fond of Iris and they would not welcome the news.

"Well, Melia? Have another half to help you make up your mind," said Glad Cheek, pushing a glass of stout towards her.

"Why pick on me?" she asked.

"Because you're a Tagg, my dear," said Princess Potter. "Ascot was first in the

166

Yard, so it's fitting her daughter should do it."

"No! Look, I'm scared of Redmayne, straight I am!"

"You scared? Come off it, Melia. A Tagg scared of anything? You're not old Ascot's daughter," said Mrs. Tilley sorrowfully.

Melia looked from one to the other. "All right, then," she said at last. "I'll do it, but it'll be for Tom's sake—that's the only reason. I'd do a lot more than that to keep the business going for him."

"Right, then. Let's go," said Mrs. Tilley.

"What, now?" gasped Melia.

"'Course now," said Ascot, who had been keeping out of the argument. "Strike while the iron's hot."

Princess Potter had just placed another glass of stout in front of Ascot and to emphasize her point the old lady drew in a deep breath and sent its thick head of foam scudding through the air to land neatly on the top of Mrs. Tilley's glass.

"See that!" she cried delightedly. "I been wanting to do that for years. That's a good omen, you see if it isn't!"

"You may think so," said Mrs. Tilley with frigid politeness, "but I say it's just plain vulgar."

She removed the extra head of foam with a teaspoon which she took out of her handbag, then she drank her stout, stood up and adjusted her hat and declared herself ready to go.

"We can all go in the van," she declared grandly.

But when they were outside and saw the van Melia panicked. The very sight of Cyril Redmayne made her legs turn to water and whenever he drove into the Yard she trembled inwardly. It was a fear she could not explain or control. Yet she loved the Yard and shrank from the idea of leaving it. It was her whole life and it was essential to keep their pitch there so as to have something for Tom when he came home.

That was why it was up to her to tackle Cyril Redmayne and there were the Tilleys all ready to drive her to do battle, they were exhorting her to buck up and get in. But she could not go now, not tonight, smelling of beer and not in her best. Tomorrow. Sunday. She would feel more in the mood on Sunday. When she put it to the others they agreed after very little argument that perhaps it was a good idea.

All next morning Melia was on tenter-hooks and when Johnny called for Iris in the afternoon she wondered if he was actually quieter than usual or if his air of preoccupation was simply a reflection of her own mood.

"Anything wrong?" she asked.

"No, everything's fine," he said.

But things were far from fine because he had just had a scene with his father which he could not tell her about. He had known the whole morning that things were bound to come to a head soon for the atmosphere at home had been tense.

They lunched in silence and after coffee, which they took at the table, he rose and went towards the door. Cyril asked him where he was going. Johnny said he was going out for a bit.

"Where?" demanded Cyril.

In the ordinary way Johnny would have told him but the tone of his father's voice dried up his responsiveness and he could not bring himself to say he was going to see Maurice Royal with Iris.

"Look here, Dad——" he protested, but Cyril cut in with:

"Are you going to see that Crockett girl?"

"Yes," said Johnny, and then he added with a touch of bravado: "Have you any objection?"

He realized at once that it was the most foolish thing he could have said, but he never dreamed it would cause his father to launch into such a tirade against the people of Sparrow's Yard and the Crocketts in particular. He literally flinched from the avalanche of abuse for Cyril Redmayne was almost beside himself with fury.

"You're being damned unfair," he said, when his father paused at last. "You might at least take the trouble to get to know Iris. Let me bring her home."

"I'd as soon you brought a ferret home," barked Cyril. "There's only one thing for you to do, my boy. Drop that girl—and quickly."

"But you don't understand. I love her."

"Love!" Cyril gave a harsh cackle of laughter that made Johnny go quite cold. "Love," he repeated. "You don't even know her."

"I know her enough to want to marry her," Johnny said, struggling to keep his voice firm and strong.

"Marry? A slut from a lemon basket! You're out of your mind. You're infatuated."

"I'm sorry, Dad. I mean it. I'm going to marry Iris as soon as it's possible."

"I forbid it," Cyril said.

"But you can't. Hang it all, I'm twenty-one!"

Cyril was silent for what seemed an interminable time. Then he said quietly: "Very well, my boy. But I warn you. I shall put a stop to this foolishness, so don't try me too far."

He rose from the table and sat by the fire with his hands behind his head and his eyes closed, as though the subject had been dismissed, and after a moment's hesitation Johnny left the room and walked down to Lantern Place.

Inwardly he was boiling. The insults his father had hurled at Iris and her family had almost stunned him and he could not see that his attitude was ever likely to change.

Yet there was nothing his father could

do to keep them apart. They had already decided they would wait till times were more propitious before they married, but during that time he had hoped to be able to ease the weight of her responsibilities. He had hoped his father might gradually come round to the idea of accepting her but now he had to dismiss the idea.

Iris had sensed this hostility from the first and now he appreciated her fear, but he did not share it. He was determined not to allow anything to prevent him from marrying her but his usual optimism was dashed and he realized it would be unfair not to tell her how matters stood.

He tried to shake off his depression and at least to sound lively when he reached Lantern Place, but he thought Melia gave him a rather searching look.

"Give Maurice my love," she said, as they were leaving. "I expect you'll be talking music."

"I shouldn't wonder," Iris replied. "What are you going to do?"

"Oh, I shall be all right," said Melia. "I might even go for a walk seeing it's such a nice afternoon."

"Walk!" chuckled Iris. "You'll be

asleep round the fire five minutes after we've gone."

But Iris was wrong, for as soon as they left the house Melia squeezed into her tightest roll-on, donned her gaudy red dress, her imitation fur coat and her best hat. She crammed her feet into flimsy, stiletto-heeled shoes and with good luck wishes from Ascot and Camille she made her way to the Redmaynes' house, which was set high on the hill above Villa Park.

She could not remember ever having approached such a house before and her courage almost failed her as she stood before the huge, heavy front door looking at the knocker and trying to summon up the will power to raise it. At last she gave a loud single knock.

Inside Helen Redmayne heard it and was thankful for the diversion. The scene between Cyril and Johnny after lunch had disturbed her deeply and she wished with all her heart they had never gone to the Villa. The controlled way in which Cyril had told her he meant to put a stop to the affair between Johnny and Iris after meeting them there had really frightened her.

173

So when she heard the knock she was glad to escape from the room where she had been sitting with Cyril, but the sight of Melia Crockett on the step did not allay her fears. The woman was dressed for a state visit and Helen felt a surge of pity for her. That terrible hat and those pathetic shoes!

Melia Crockett was breathing heavily and if Cyril had been out Helen would have given her a cup of tea. As it was she just waited for her visitor to speak.

"I wonder if Mr. Redmayne could spare me a minute or two?" Melia asked timidly. "I've called on behalf of the Sparrow's Yard stallholders."

"You could hardly have chosen a worse time," Helen thought, and aloud she said: "My husband's rather tired. Perhaps it would be better to make an appointment and see him in business hours."

She was trying to help, but the woman looked so flustered and unhappy and said again that the others had asked her to call that she asked her to wait in the panelled reception room by the front door.

Melia sat nervously on the edge of a chair, gripping her handbag so hard that

174

her hands ached and straining her ears for the sound of approaching footsteps. She wished there were a looking glass so that she might at least draw confidence from the sight of her mirrored hat. She sat with her feet apart and she kept drawing her heels out of her shoes and screwing up her eyes at the agony of this temporary relief. It was a cold day but she was uncomfortably hot and she knew her face was flushed.

She did not have to wait long for Cyril Redmayne and when he came in she stood up awkwardly and said, "Pleased to see you, I'm sure."

He inclined his head slightly and replied: "I understand you have come on behalf of the Sparrow's Yard people. You are Mrs. Crockett, I believe?"

"That's right," Melia said. "I keep the vegetable stall that my mother used to have. Ascot Tagg she is—no doubt you'll remember her—and then there's my Uncle Wally, he helps out and keeps the shell-fish stall Saturdays."

"Yes, yes," Cyril said impatiently, "but what do you want to see me about?"

"Well, seeing as there's to be an office

block built and there's rumours that the Yard's going to be turned into a car park we've all been wondering what our position is," Melia said. "Naturally we're all very grateful to you for allowing us to stay on now that the old doctor's gone . . ."

"Well?" queried Cyril as she hesitated.

"Well, seeing as the chestnut tree's been cut down and there's bound to be a lot of changes, Mrs. Tilley—she has the fruit stall—and Mrs. Potter and the Cheek girls, we all thought we should get the position clear, seeing as there are bound to be changes."

"Yes, there will be changes," agreed Cyril. "Demolition and construction always cause a good deal of dust and dirt and confusion, so the Yard won't be such a comfortable place as it has been for some time to come—you must understand that."

"Oh, of course," said Melia. "We all expect that. Our concern is can we stay there when the building's done? We all love the Yard and we've been together a long time all us stallholders, but if you have other plans for the Yard—if it's really to be a car park . . ."

She tailed off uncertainly, for if the Yard were indeed to be taken from them she had no idea what they would do and she wished she knew how she could move him to pity their plight.

"You say there are five stalls in the Yard now, including your uncle's fish stall?" he asked.

"That's right," she agreed.

"How many people depend upon it, then?"

"Well, Mrs. Potter's alone now—that's one. Then there's the three Tilleys, Mr. and Mrs. and Alfie, only Mr. Tilley's an invalid. There's Winnie and Glad Cheek, single girls they are—very respectable—there's Uncle Wally and there's my family. There's three of us and my mother takes a share so that makes four."

"Then there are eleven in all," he said. "And I expect you'd be hard put to it if you had to go?"

"We should indeed. Fact is, I don't know where we'd turn, because there's not a pitch to be had in Villa Park that I know of. And us all being together, well, one draws trade to the other, like."

"And yet you'll agree that the Yard would make an excellent car park, won't you? And with the new offices it will be almost a necessity." His tone was reasonable.

"I see that, but this is our living," Melia replied. "After all, we're people and the other is just—well—motor cars."

"You realize that I lose a great deal by allowing you to stay, I hope," said Cyril. "This arrangement is most inconvenient—and distasteful, too."

"We always try to keep the Yard nice," Melia replied.

"Yes," he rapped out impatiently, "but you're enquiring about my plans for the Yard and if they are to include your stalls I want value for the concession."

"If you'll let us know what you want I'm sure we'll do our best to meet you," Melia said hopefully, for she felt the interview was going well.

"I'll tell you what it is now and make no bones about it, Mrs. Crockett," he said, for quite suddenly he saw his son's love affair and the situation in the Yard in one piece. Unconsciously the boy had handed him his weapon and here it was like a knife in his hand, all nice and sharp and ready to use. The arrival of Amelia Arethusa Crockett in her atrocious Sunday best could not have been more fortuitious.

"You have a very pretty daughter," he said, and paused.

"Indeed I have," replied Melia proudly. "My Iris is at the Abbeyfield Technical College."

"I've met her, and she does you great credit," he replied.

His cutting tone was in marked contrast with his words, yet she still felt she was making some headway, for he had been more amiable than she had expected.

"I have a son, Mrs. Crockett," he said, "and my son seems to be infatuated with your daughter. He's just told me in so many words that he wants to marry her."

"Marry!" echoed Melia. "I can't hardly believe it. Are you sure?"

"That's what he said."

"That'll be bad news to you," said Melia slowly. "I know you never cared for us people in the Yard. I suppose you'll be forbidding it?"

"My son is of age. He can do as he pleases," Cyril said shortly.

"Iris never told me. I think there must be some mistake," Melia replied.

"I assure you that my son made his intentions quite clear," Cyril repeated.

"Well then, I don't see there's much you can do," she said. "It doesn't look as though you can forbid it."

"You miss my point, Mrs. Crockett," he rapped out. "I can't forbid my son, but you can forbid your daughter. Now do you see?"

"I daresay I can. But why should I?" Melia demanded, stung to a sudden, angry defiance. "This is all news to me, but why should I be the one to stand in the way of two young people that's in love?"

"I'll tell you why," he said. "You keep your girl away from my boy and you stall people can keep your pitches in my yard. Now do you understand?"

Melia stared at him disbelievingly. "You can't mean it," she said at last. "You'd never treat your own child like that!"

"I'd do more to stop him ruining his life," Cyril answered. "I mean what I say, Mrs. Crockett. It's up to you now."

She had to grip the arms of the chair she had sunk into and her voice was no more than a croak.

"You always hated us but not so much as this, for pity's sake," she said.

Her words were not so much a cry for mercy as the measure of her incredulity. That she should conspire with the man who hated her against her own child was diabolical.

"Think it over," he said. "I'm treating you pretty handsomely, all told. I could have you out tomorrow—the pack of you —and you'd have no redress. You've no rights, my good woman, so don't delude yourself. As it is I'm offering you the freedom of the Yard. It's a sensible offer, a generous one. You'd better take it."

He seemed to tower above her and she stared up dumbly, her voice paralysed in her throat.

"Just see your daughter breaks off whatever kind of affair they're having and breaks it off properly," he said. "I don't want any of these filthy cuddling parties that lead to nothing but squalling brats. So do as I say and you'll be all right. All eleven of you."

She almost choked with anger and she could not think clearly or speak coherently but the need to make some kind of protest was too strong to deny. Yet all she could do was to rail in a harsh, grating voice, knowing that with every word she uttered she lost a little more of her dignity.

Cyril watched her, a flicker of cold amusement on his face, just as though he were observing an unpleasant reptile, a slimy thing from under a stone, from a safe distance. When she had no more words left he said contemptuously, "I see we understand each other perfectly, Mrs. Crockett, so if you have no more to say I'll wish you good afternoon."

With that he left the room, flung the front door open and departed, leaving her to make her bewildered way out of the house alone.

13

MELIA could never remember how she got home after she stumbled down the steps of the Redmayne house. Her mind was in a tumult, for not only her own family's future but the future of all her friends in the Yard depended on her, or rather upon Iris, and she was bemused by the injustice of it.

Whether or not Iris cared for Johnny seemed outside the question to her: the fact that one man had such power over the lives of eleven people outweighed everything else and there was no denying that this was the position, yet try as she might she could not see a solution to their problem. If she did not fall in with Mr. Redmayne's wishes what would the Tilleys and the Cheeks and Princess Potter do? There was nowhere else for them to trade. Every licensed pitch in Villa Park was held by one or other of the Perks family and there were no altruistic people like Dr. Redmayne left.

She thought of Tom. She must have something for him to come home to and her main object in life had been to keep the stall going ever since he had been taken away. She prayed wordlessly as she made her way home in the hope that help would come and yet she could not see any possibility of it. She was tottering along in her high-heeled, flimsy shoes and when she reached the High Road she could bear them no longer, so she took them off and continued in her stockinged feet. Somehow the shoes seemed to magnify her sense of failure and despair.

"I was afraid your feet would play you up," Camille said when Melia got in. Then she saw the look on her sister's face and knew there was something much worse the matter. Melia's eyes were red and her gaunt face had a yellowish hue and she trembled convulsively as though she had suffered a shock.

It took some time for the family to find out what had passed between her and Cyril Redmayne and when they knew they reacted to the news in their own individual ways.

"Our Iris don't want nothing to do with that Johnny!" declared Uncle Wally angrily. "I've said so all along. He's not good enough for her to wipe her boots on. I'd like to punch his head, I would."

"What do you want to go punching Johnny's head for?" demanded Ascot. "Far better go and punch his father's— he's the one who's causing all the trouble."

"There's no sense in blaming the wrong person," agreed Camille. "It's a wicked shame this should happen."

"What are we to do, though?" demanded Melia. "There's the Tilleys to think of. They'd be in a proper mess if they had to go, and what about us? What do we live on? Don't think I haven't enquired about another pitch because I have and there's nowhere in Villa Park today."

"That dratted Tom ought to be here," complained Ascot. "He should be taking his share of the trouble and not leaving it all to his mother."

"Say what you like, they've only known each other five minutes," Wally remarked in a bad-tempered voice. "Anyone would think they were being parted at the altar. Met Christmas Eve, didn't they? They're just a couple of kids and they'll have forgotten each other in a week."

"That's what you think," said Camille, bridling. "Much you know about love, Uncle Wally!"

"But what am I to do?" asked Melia. "Give her my blessing and some orange blossom and the sack for everyone else?"

"You'll have to tell her the way things are," said Ascot, who had remained silent for some time. "She'll have to face it."

"If she'd been a flighty girl and had lots of boys it wouldn't have been so bad," said Melia miserably. "Still, she'll be back at college Tuesday and her time'll be taken up with study from now till summer. Perhaps she'll cool off."

"You may pull the wool over your own eyes, but you don't pull it over mine," said Camille. "Johnny wants to marry her and he's told his father so and now old Cyril's put the ball in your court good and proper."

"Can you think of anything different to do?" asked Melia.

"I haven't put my mind to it yet," said Camille.

"Then for goodness' sake put your mind to it now and tell me the answer," implored Melia.

But although Camille puzzled and pondered and tried to find a way out she was defeated at every turn and when Iris came in a little later on they were still in the same confused state as when Melia first told them Cyril Redmayne's terms.

"Well!" exclaimed Iris from the doorway as she viewed her assembled family with some apprehension. "Whatever's the matter with you all? Have you had bad news or something?"

"Not specially good," Ascot replied.

"Where have you been?" demanded Melia belligerently. "Don't tell me you've been at Maurice's all this time. I expected you long ago."

"I've been in the coffee bar with Johnny," Iris said.

"Doing what?"

"Goodness me, what would you think? Talking, of course," Iris said nervously.

The day had turned out so differently from how she had expected. They spent a pleasant, rather exciting afternoon with Maurice and she had been glad to take a back seat and listen to the two men discussing Johnny's songs. But afterwards, on the way home, Johnny had confirmed her fears about his father's antagonism and this had led to endless speculation.

"Now don't you sauce me, young lady," blared Melia, venting her own unhappiness on Iris. "I think you're seeing a good deal too much of that Johnny Redmayne and I don't know that I like it. You're not the same girl since you've been going out with him and I reckon you'd be wise to give up seeing him."

"Ma! Whatever do you mean?" gasped Iris.

"What I say," returned Melia. "He may be a nice enough young fellow in his way but I don't want you mixed up with that Redmayne crowd."

"It's a bit late to tell me that because I *am* mixed up with him now," Iris said. "He's asked me to marry him."

"When did he ask you?"

"Saturday . . ."

"And you wait till now to tell me? You

could have warned me, Iris. I don't know how you could treat me like this!"

"Not this minute!" Iris cried. "Not for years and years maybe—he understands the way things are, but he asked me and I've told him yes, so there's nothing you can do about it because we love each other. Truly we do."

No one spoke and she gazed from one to the other and they all looked like strangers.

"Ma!" she said in a little, trembling voice. "Ma!"

Melia could not see Iris properly because her eyes were swimming with tears and in a sudden gesture of defeat she hid her face in her arms and her shoulders shook with sobs. Iris was at her side in a second, kneeling with her arms round her, begging her not to worry and telling her that everything would be all right and she would not think of leaving her yet. Johnny would not ask her to.

Camille and Ascot exchanged glances and Wally lit his pipe and drew on it noisily, making ugly bubbling noises and filling the room with smoke.

"There's something you're not telling me," said Iris. "Is it Tom?"

Melia shook her head and Iris knew instinctively that Mr. Redmayne had taken some kind of action. She could almost feel his presence. He was in Sparrow's Yard, he had been in Lantern Place, he controlled their lives and their futures.

It was not long before she learned the truth and it frightened her terribly. The knowledge that their livelihood and that of their friends rested on her decision was unbearable, but there was no doubt of it. They were completely in Cyril Redmayne's power—all of them—and he would not hesitate to use it. Johnny had said enough to convince her of that.

"But why?" she kept asking. "Why should he treat us like this? Maybe he did hope Johnny would fall for someone better, but we love each other! Perhaps he'll understand if we tell him."

"No. It'd be like beating a granite wall with your bare fists. You'd only bleed the more, my dearie," Melia said. "Best forget Johnny."

"Forget? How could I?" Iris cried, and she clung to her hopes against all arguments. She clung to them all through that night of fitful sleep and during the next long day. Hope kept springing up in spite of all Melia had told her. She could not believe that in the space of a few minutes she had lost so much.

Now, as never before, she felt trapped in the close knit fabric of her family and the fellowship of the Yard. She was woven into it like a design and she could no more extricate herself than a printed flower can tear itself from the material in which it is enmeshed and yet remain whole.

"I can't give him up—I won't," she thought desperately, but she knew in her heart that the future she had seen stretching away before her in a golden haze was already a grey waste which she would have to traverse alone.

That evening when Johnny came to Lantern Place she was waiting for him under the lamp and as he flung his arms round her she clung to him with all her strength. It was a bitterly cold night and his face felt like ice.

"What's the matter?" he asked, for he could feel her trembling as he held her.

"Ma went to see your father about the

Yard while we were at Maurice's," she said, "and he's made her forbid us to see each other. I can't even ask you in."

"Not see each other?" he echoed in a tone of disbelief. "Why not? What's it all about?"

"He's determined to keep us apart," she said, and she told him what had happened. "Is he really as ruthless as that?" she asked.

"He is at the moment," Johnny said. "I never guessed he'd go quite so far, though. He was pretty ghastly to me."

"What shall we do?" she asked.

"We shall have to be patient and wear him down," he said after a pause, for he did not know how to answer her and he had nothing but his own determination to help him.

"But it could go on for ever," she said.

"Do you remember telling me you wanted to help your mother and I said I'd help her too?" he asked. "This is the only way we can do it. I love you enough to go weeks without seeing you so long as I know you love me."

"You know I do," she said.

"I want to be with you more than

anything in the world and I don't care how long I have to wait," he said. "It's going to be miserable, but if we did anything to damage the Yard people we'd never be able to live with ourselves afterwards. We can't escape that."

"When I think of days and weeks and months without seeing you I don't know how I shall bear it, though," she said.

"I'll be there. I'll be around. We've just got to hang on," he said. "We'll win in the end. Come on—let's face it."

"I don't know how!" she cried. "It's been such heaven—you can't guess what heaven it's been!"

"But I can. I was there too, remember? Listen, we won't plan the future—we'll just believe in it and I'll walk through Sparrow's Yard every Saturday just to see you're there."

"I shall live for Saturdays," she said.

"I'll send you roses every Monday so you'll know I'm thinking of you."

"Oh, Johnny, you are wonderful! But what can I do for you?" she asked.

"Keep your chin up and don't give way," he told her. "We're going to get married, so don't ever give up. I promise faithfully that I won't."

"I promise too," she said.

But Johnny thought long and deeply after he left her. He weighed up all the forces his father could bring to bear against them and his conclusions were discouraging. He could not see how they were ever to extricate themselves from their dilemma.

The only way he could protest against his father's threat would be to leave home, but on consideration he decided against this. It would be unpleasant there, but at least he would be on the scene; he would be able to observe his father's movements and reactions and gauge his mood. It would be like keeping a finger on the pulse of things.

When he told Iris that he could be patient he was not exaggerating, but he feared he was going to have to exercise this virtue to the limit.

14

IRIS should have returned to college the following day, but during the night Melia was ill. Her interview with Cyril Redmayne had completely unnerved her and Aunt Camille thought the last part of her journey home without her shoes had given her a chill. She coughed and shivered and ran a high temperature.

"It's the 'flu," Ascot pronounced. "No Sparrow's Yard for you today, my girl."

"'Flu? Me?" croaked Melia indignantly. "Never heard such rubbish. Here, I'm getting up. I can't afford to be ill."

"You're not getting up," Ascot said. "I'll go down to the Yard myself. Don't worry. The place won't fall down without you."

Iris had just brought in a tray with tea for her mother and she was in time to hear the argument.

"You're not either of you going," she said. "I'm going myself. It won't matter

195

missing a couple of days at the Tech. I can get someone else's notes."

"Well, I never did!" exclaimed Melia. "Who are you to say what you will and will not do? You go along off to school. I never heard such goings-on in my life."

Iris sat down and began to comb her hair in front of her mother's mirror.

"I'm not a little girl," she said, "so please don't treat me as though I am. You're ill and Gran's old and Uncle Wally can't do everything by himself. That leaves me. We can't afford to let the stall go even for a day. Besides, I'd like to go."

Melia sank back on her pillows with an exclamation of surprise. She had never seen such a determined look on her daughter's face before and although she still pretended displeasure she felt an inward glow of thankfulness.

"Kids! I don't know who'd have 'em!" she exclaimed. "First Tom and now you, Iris. You'll worry me into an early grave."

"Left it a bit late, haven't you?" chuckled Ascot. "Here, you stay comfortable, Melia, and I'll fetch you a couple of hot-water bottles."

She left the room and soon afterwards

Iris went down to the Yard, much to the surprise of Uncle Wally, who had not expected to see anyone, least of all his niece.

They set out the stall between them and Iris lugged sacks of sprouts and onions from the storehouse, and rolled out barrels of carrots and handled crates full of freezing wet spinach. The day was overcast and the clouds low-lying, so that the cold, damp air smelt of smoke and diesel fumes.

Work had begun on the Redmayne site and a fiendish machine that reminded Iris of a dragon was tearing over the ground clawing up the shrubs and destroying the hedge with the briar rose growing over it. Whenever Uncle Wally caught sight of the demolition men he muttered and swore under his breath and Dook, sensing his master's uneasiness, whinnyed loudly from inside the stable and stamped his hooves and showed signs of restlessness.

"Dook knows," Uncle Wally said. "You don't have to tell him nothing."

At midday he led the horse out into the Yard to let him see a bit of life, as he put it, but in reality he did this for the sake of the schoolchildren who never missed stopping to gaze at him on their way along the High Road. They trickled along in twos and threes till presently the cry "Dook's out!" brought hoards of small girls and boys into the Yard carrying lumps of sugar to give him or else begging Iris for carrots.

"How old is he?" they asked.

"Never you mind," returned Wally huffily, for Dook's age was a sore point with him.

"What's he called Dook for?"

"'Cos it was the Dook of Villa Park gave him to me. Never heard of him, did you? Iggerant, that's what you are. What do they teach you at school?"

But Uncle Wally's taciturn manner deceived no one but himself and he basked in the warmth of Dook's reflected glory and his old eyes looked kindly on the children.

During a slack period Iris left the stall and telephoned Mrs. Drew to explain her absence. The teacher was concerned when she heard what had happened since her conversation with Iris on the last day of term.

"I shall do my best to see you don't

suffer through having to be away," she said. "I hope you've got warm clothes on—you don't want to catch cold yourself."

"I couldn't be warmer—I look as though I'm bound for the North Pole," Iris said.

"Well, at least you sound cheerful."

Much to her own surprise Iris found that she was not feeling nearly so despondent as she had expected and she realized that working in the Yard was having its usual magical effect on her in spite of the presence of demolition men and the noise of their work.

There had been the usual exchange of greetings with the other stallholders and many good wishes and messages for her mother. There had been the mugs of cocoa from Mrs. Tilley, offers of a swig of stout out of the bottle from Glad Cheek, a ham sandwich from Princess Potter. And they had all given her things for Ma. She had flowers and a bunch of grapes and as the Cheek sisters did not think an invalid would fancy salad they gave her a flagon of burgundy to take home.

"A glass of that with an egg beat up in

it will do her the world of good," advised Winnie. "Our mum always swore by it."

Iris thanked her and suppressed a smile. Winnie and Glad were always referred to as girls but they were not far short of sixty. They both liked to flirt with Uncle Wally and often threatened to marry him if he didn't watch out.

"I'm watching," he would say.

"Poor old trouts," said Iris.

Uncle Wally looked indignant. "Who are you calling a trout?" he asked. "Very pretty young ladies, Winnie and Glad. They'd knock spots off you, my girl. Here, pick up that spinach leaf you dropped. Don't want me breaking my neck, do you?"

The first day passed quickly and Iris was exhausted by the time she got home. She had done a full day's work and had lugged and pushed and lifted almost as strenuously as Melia did. It was not till she was home that she could think of Johnny peacefully and now she felt that she must match her spirits with his. Somehow she must make herself share his faith in their future and fight the depression which so often threatened to engulf her.

Working in the Yard that week was a tremendous help. Friday was a busy day and she told Aunt Camille she would have some lunch at a nearby café so as to lose as little time as possible from the stall. She rather enjoyed it and was finishing with a cup of tea when she felt someone was watching her and saw it was Raymond Perks. He was alone at the next table and suddenly he leaned across and offered her a cigarette from his packet.

"Thanks, but I don't smoke," she said.

"Mind if I sit here?" he asked, moving his seat to one opposite hers.

"Not in the least, though I can't think why you want to change," she said. "Your table looks just as good as this one."

He puffed out some smoke and waved it away. "Don't seem to be able to make smoke rings. Been trying for years," he said. Then he leaned across the table. "We don't always have to go on as though we're strangers, do we, Iris?" he asked.

"I don't see we can behave like bosom friends," she replied.

"Look. We're brother and sister. I seen you working in the Yard all this week, so I know there's something wrong."

"It's only because Ma's ill. She'll be back tomorrow," answered Iris. "She just had a touch of 'flu."

"I wish that was all my mother had," remarked Raymond.

Iris kept a stony silence. Any ill that befell Florrie Perks just served her right.

"I know what you're thinking," he said. "But Selina and me didn't have much fun either, Iris. I don't suppose you ever thought of that, did you? It was hell when Dad walked out and didn't come back. We never knew but that him and Mum were married."

"Oh," she said. "I didn't ever think of that. It didn't cross my mind."

"Haven't got much imagination, have you? I reckon you must be quite a hard little thing."

"Me hard? I'm not!" she exclaimed indignantly. "I'd do anything for Ma, or for any of my people."

"Well, I'd do anything for mine, so we can call it quits," he said. "Only I been thinking it's about time you admitted Selina and me's your people, too. We had the same father—let's leave the mothers out of it. Let them feud if they want to, there's no reason why we should. There's enough trouble without us adding to it. It can't be a picnic in the Yard just now."

"Goodness, you're right," she agreed sadly.

"Well, all I want to say is that any time you need help don't forget I'm around. I can hump your potatoes and cart your crates any time."

She made herself look straight at him and found herself gazing into a pair of eyes that were as blue and brilliant as ever Quick Crockett's had been.

"You're ever so generous, Raymond. I do appreciate it," she said softly.

He smiled and put his hand over hers for a brief second. Then he got up and lounged out, hunching his shoulders inside his leather jacket. She noticed the rather pathetic swagger of his exit and a wave of inexpressible tenderness swept over her. Suddenly she felt the emotions he had tried to express and she saw him small and bewildered and bereft of his father. She saw him as he looked when he used to beg for a ride on Dook and she saw his hopefulness turn to defiance when he was refused. She could almost hear the echo of his atrocious, unquenchable Perks' voice —"Yah! Beaver! Get your face shaved!"

"Goodness, I'm lucky," she thought. "I've had nothing but love and kindness all my life."

When she finished at the Yard that evening and hurried home, leaving Uncle Wally at the Duke's Head to console himself with a pint, she had another surprise in store. She met Johnny.

She had just turned into the road approaching the alley when she saw him coming and for a moment she could not believe her eyes. She stood still, half afraid.

"Johnny!"

She ran forward and then stopped. "Suppose someone sees us?" she said.

"Who?" he asked, as he swept her into his arms. "You didn't tell me you weren't going to be at Abbeyfield this week."

"Ma's been ill, so I've been helping Uncle Wally," she told him. "Gran calls it 'flu, but I think it's the shock and sheer misery of Sunday. Coming home without her shoes on the cold pavement, too."

"Without her shoes? Whatever for?"

"Oh, it was just that she wore her best

ones to look nice seeing your father and her feet always hurt anyway and—oh Johnny!—you can't think how awful all this has been for Ma."

Somehow she made him feel the utter humiliation of Amelia Crockett and he experienced an almost unbearable sense of pity as he thought of the gaunt faced woman in the ill-chosen clothes and imagined her facing his father.

He held Iris closer and the material of her old coat felt coarse and grimy under his hands. Her scarf was damp from her breath and her face looked white and cold. At that moment he wanted to throw his furled umbrella over the roof tops and hump sacks of potatoes for her till he dropped from sheer exhaustion. He wanted to share the cold of the Yard with her, he wanted to know the feeling of having his feet almost freeze to the pavement, he wanted to taste Mrs. Tilley's thick cocoa and exchange backchat with Glad and Winnie. He wanted so desperately to help.

He took his fur-lined gloves out of his pocket and drew them on to her hands. They were so large they almost fell off.

"I'll send you a pair that fit tomorrow," he said.

She stood on tiptoe and kissed him. "Darling Johnny," she said, and she did not have the heart to say that she already possessed two pairs of good gloves but that she could not wear them to serve vegetables and count out change.

"I'd better go in, Uncle Wally will be coming," she said. "Oh, but it's been so wonderful seeing you."

As they walked towards the alley he told her that Maurice had been in touch with him again. "He wants to see some more of my stuff and he asked me to drop in again sometime," he said.

"Do you suppose he might sing one of your songs himself? Just imagine if he did!" she exclaimed.

"There's no suggestion of that," Johnny said.

"Well, Aunt Camille's absolutely sold on you and Maurice must think you're good or he'd never bother."

"It's nice to be encouraged. A bit frightening, though. Look, I won't come any further. I'll wait here till you get through the alley. Shout out when you're in Lantern Place."

Iris hated the alley, especially the dark patch in the middle where no lamplight reached, but with Johnny so near she felt safe and she was buoyed up by their wonderful, forbidden meeting.

"Good night," she called, in her clear, sweet voice, and she heard Johnny's answer ring out strong and true.

"Who were you calling out to?" asked Aunt Camille when she opened the door.

"Just a friend," said Iris airily.

Aunt Camille laughed. "Nice to have friends who make your eyes sparkle," she said. "Life's not so bad, is it?"

15

IRIS went back to Abbeyfield on Monday.

"Had a good holiday?" the girls asked.

She hesitated and then said fervently: "Marvellous! Simply marvellous!"

She was not exaggerating. In that short holiday she had fallen in love, come up against the full barrage of Mr. Redmayne's wrath and discovered that no amount of threats could alter her feelings. She would never have believed that so much could happen in so short a time and after her initial distress at Mr. Redmayne's behaviour and her anxiety over her mother she had got her second wind and could face the difficulties that beset her inspired by her love for Johnny.

Although he never came to Lantern Place now he contrived occasional meetings which were all the more thrilling because of the element of risk. Sometimes she would find him waiting in the dark, furtive alley where the ground was strewn with litter and greasy newspapers and they would kiss and cling together, the sweetness of their meeting sharpened by its brevity.

At other long intervals they met in the darkness of a coffee bar near Abbeyfield and they would sit close together, their arms about each other, their voices drowned by the noise of the incessant pop music. Through the blare he would try to croon her his latest song but this brought protests from the amorous couples on either side so he would give her a sheet of manuscript to take home and play over with Aunt Camille.

He was putting all his energy into his music now, working every night at home, occasionally calling on Maurice and coming away from him deflated by his criticism but never daunted. Iris, too, threw herself into her work for they both felt that the harder they worked the nearer they would come to solving their problem and she had an ally in Aunt Camille, for she felt safe in confiding in her.

One evening, not long after the spring term had begun, Aunt Camille came home from a visit to Maurice's flat bubbling over with excitement and she beckoned Iris into the kitchen.

"What do you think? Maurice has introduced Johnny to young Reub Hillstein!"

"Not *the* Hillstein?" gasped Iris.

"Yes! The one who wrote the lyrics for *The Silver Staircase*. He's done a lyric for Johnny's tune—'The Old Songs'! What do you say to that?"

"Oh, Auntie, it's marvellous. Reub Hillstein!" she exclaimed. "How I wish I'd been to see Maurice with you! What are the words?"

"I don't know. I only got the bit of news. Isn't that enough for you?" Camille asked.

"Not nearly. Oh, you might have found out!"

"Well, I wish I had. Still, Maurice will be here tomorrow and he'll sing it to you."

"I don't know how to wait. I ought to have gone with you," Iris said.

"That wouldn't have done at all," Camille replied slyly. "Johnny happened to be there."

"You never told me! Oh, Auntie, how

210

can you be so mean? How did he look and what did he say?"

"They talked a lot about music really, dear. I was a bit out of it. Maurice and Johnny get on like one o'clock."

"What else did they talk about? You make it sound so prosaic, Auntie."

"Johnny sent you this," Camille said, giving Iris a little packet wrapped in tissue paper, "and his love and kisses and to say he thinks you're looking fine and he fairly bursts with pride every time he sees you in Sparrow's Yard," she added.

"Honestly? Is that truly what he said?"

"Honestly," replied Camille. "What's in the box?"

The box contained a pair of turquoise and marquisite ear-rings.

"Aren't they heavenly?" exclaimed Iris. "Just think—this is my first really important present from Johnny. Don't you think it's absolutely beautiful?"

"I do. They're just the colour for you. Look, there's a note with them."

The note was brief. It simply said: *A ring next time, darling*.

Iris read it over and over, then she folded it up carefully and replaced it in the box. She thought it was the most beautiful message she had ever received. She longed so much to see Johnny—just to touch his hand—and the fact that Aunt Camille had been with him only intensified this feeling.

There were times when she wanted to talk and talk about him and she was often tempted when she was with Caroline Golding who knew him so well and who had remarked on his attraction to her at the Christmas party.

"He really was smitten with you, Iris," she declared. "I've known him since we were kids and I can tell just how he feels. The Redmaynes have got pots of money, you know. Why, I expect you could be married right away if you really fell for him."

"What on?" asked Iris. "I shouldn't think he's the kind who'd live on his father's money."

"No, he's frightfully independent, but old Daddy Redmayne would be bound to help. Anyone with all that lolly would, wouldn't they?"

"I don't know," said Iris, "and as I never see Johnny I don't think it matters."

"You'd make a simply lovely pair,"

Caroline remarked sentimentally, "and think what beautiful children you'd have."

Iris was torn between her desire to hear more and her fear that Caroline would get to know too much.

"I thought Mr. Redmayne was very stand-offish," she said.

"Oh well, he can't help that. My mother told me he had an unhappy childhood."

"What kind of a childhood did he have, then?" asked Iris, eager to hear somebody else's version of it.

"He had a perfectly awful, dotty old father. I think he was a doctor—one of these terrible do-gooders. His father didn't marry till he was in his dotage and Mr. Redmayne's mother had a dreadful time. He took her to live in his beastly old house and you'll never guess what she had to put up with in her very own front garden."

Caroline paused, and Iris, who was beginning to feel a hot flush discolouring her neck, said in a croaky voice, "What?"

"A whole lot of awful old vegetable barrows with dirty old barrow men and women turning the place into a market! They really were the dregs, Iris. It sounds funny now but there was one old girl who never took the curlers out of her hair and she used to call Mr. Redmayne 'cock'. I should think he must have been ever such a prim little boy and she used to say, ''Morning, little cock.' What's the matter?''

"It's hot in here. I'm stifled," Iris said.

They had the classroom to themselves, for it was break, and Caroline had dashed in for a hurried chat. She opened the window and said, "Johnny's not a bit like his father, you know."

"Thank God for that," said Iris. "His father sounds unbearable."

"Oh, only a bit stuffy," said Caroline. "After all, things that happen in childhood do affect you."

"You just said all his money should make up for it," Iris reminded her. "What else happened to make him sour?"

"His mother couldn't stand the way his father went on—he had patients filling up the house till all hours and then there were these barrow people outside—so she left him."

"And what became of all those filthy barrow people?" asked Iris savagely.

"Goodness knows, I don't," said

Caroline lightly. "There, I must fly. Guess what? I'm going to perm Mrs. Drew. See you."

She danced out of the classroom, leaving Iris to grip the desk and dig her fingernails into the wood in an effort to control her anger.

Dirty old barrow men and women! They were her people, her own people, and her heart and soul cried out against the insult. To think that anyone should dare to call Ascot dirty and laugh at her hair curlers when she had stood out there wet, fine, cold or dry, selling vegetables first from a basket to keep body and soul together, and then from a stall.

And Uncle Wally, getting up in the mean hours of the early morning to comb and groom Dook and to make him look spanking smart to draw the cart to market. And what of the Cheek girls with their salad stall arranged in a design that would catch an artist's eye and the fruit on Mrs. Tilley's stall brightening the whole world with its colour? Sparrow's Yard was not an eyesore, it was an eruption of colour in the High Road. It was vital, glowing, alive. It was faith and hope and as she realized this Iris felt her anger melt away. She was glad she belonged to Sparrow's Yard. She was proud of it.

Suddenly she wanted Caroline Golding and all the world to know. She went to the door of the classroom in time to see Caroline parting from another student with whom she had been talking outside.

"I want you a minute," Iris said.

Caroline followed her back looking puzzled. "What's the matter?" she asked.

"I only want you to know that those people with the barrows, those filthy people who spoilt Mr. Redmayne's childhood, are my people," she said. "That awful old woman with the hair curlers is my grandmother. She still wears the curlers, if you'd like to know. My mother still keeps a vegetable stall in Sparrow's Yard. You can tell anyone you like. And when you do just say I'm proud of them."

"Oh, Iris," gasped Caroline. "I'm sorry. I'd never have said—you know I wouldn't. Oh I am sorry, truly."

"You needn't be," Iris replied. "Unless you pity yourself for thinking the way you do."

Caroline looked away miserably. She

had always liked and admired Iris Crockett and now she liked her more than ever but this explanation solved a riddle that had been puzzling her for she had been told of Mr. Redmayne's displeasure at his son's attraction to this girl who, on the surface, was so desirable.

"I only repeated what I heard," Caroline said slowly. "In future I'll judge for myself. I'm only sorry I hurt you, Iris. I'm not sorry because you belong to those people, they must be pretty wonderful to have someone like you. Don't let Mr. Redmayne break up whatever there is between you and Johnny."

"Mr. Redmayne couldn't break a soft boiled egg," said Iris scornfully. "Don't worry. He won't upset *my* life."

She spoke in this strain because she did not want anyone to guess the depth of her feeling for Johnny. Then she felt sorry for Caroline, who was just a silly, thoughtless little creature like a lovely dragonfly skimming about on the surface of life.

"You'll be late for Mrs. Drew," she said in a much softer tone. "Hope you'll give her a nice perm."

As far as work went the spring term was

speeding by much too quickly and Iris found it difficult to manage two evenings a week to practise driving the Tilleys' van.

"I do hope I pass the test, Alfie," she said. "Somehow I can't see Dook lasting out much longer."

"You'll pass all right," he said encouragingly. "You can handle this thing as well as I can already."

"I shall be thankful to get it off my chest with the exams coming along in the summer."

They were driving down a deserted road and a soft touch of spring was in the air. Alfie would have liked to get out and stroll along the grassy verge and perhaps slip his arm round her but a glance at her determined profile checked him. Although they were so close, she seemed terribly far away these days. He knew she was unattainable and he loved her more deeply than ever.

Meanwhile conditions in Sparrow's Yard were deteriorating still more. The stall-holders tried not to look when Dr. Redmayne's house was pulled down and rooms that had long been hidden suddenly gaped open as an outer wall fell. A glimpse of the striped wallpaper in the dining room made Mrs. Tilley wince. She had waited there so many long hours with Ernie when he first became ill.

No sooner had the dust subsided and the rubble been cleared away than the contractor's lorries began to rumble through the Yard daily. An enormous excavator arrived to scoop the good earth from the garden and its noise served as a background to the stallholders' anxiety, which still persisted even in the face of the assurances Melia gave them after her mission to Cyril Redmayne.

They regarded the labourers working on the site as enemies. Soon the air was full of the noise of piledrivers and huge cement mixers disgorged masses of concrete for the foundations. The heavy traffic cracked the old flagged stones of the Yard so that a shower of rain made the place muddy and when it was wet shoppers avoided it.

The wind brought clouds of dust from the site and this settled on the stalls and the Cheek girls complained because their lettuces were gritty and Mrs. Tilley sat at her stall wearing a look of indignant resignation and when the last beams of the sun fell on her black hat at the end of the day it was seen to have a white and matted look.

Melia moved her stall a little closer to the shop wall because it was no longer safe for the customers to throng the Yard as they had been used to do. Often the lorries came so close they almost touched the stalls and remonstrances brought the answer that the drivers were only doing their job.

Iris saw these difficulties clearly and she was concerned at the signs of strain in her mother's face, but sometimes, when she thought of the price they were paying to survive, she wanted to run away. It was easy to be brave when Johnny was with her, but now the evenings were growing lighter and it was not so easy to manage meetings for fear of being seen. Her glimpses of him as he walked through the Yard on Saturdays became almost exasperating.

She would wait for the moment in a state of high tension and she could scarcely pay attention to her work till he had come and gone. Then afterwards she felt so rebellious that it was almost impossible to think clearly. She muddled the change, got the orders wrong and was in such a state of confusion that she hardly knew what she was doing.

"I'm all on edge," she would say.

"Go on home and have a nice cup of tea," Melia would advise her. "You're all upset. It'd be better if that Johnny stayed away."

"It wouldn't!" Iris cried. "I'd die if I didn't just catch a glimpse of him. It's little enough, isn't it?"

Gradually this mood would pass; she would begin to see things in perspective again and to feel calmer and then she would draw strength from the knowledge of Johnny's determination. There was nothing they could do but wait.

16

JOHNNY was feeling the strain, too. It was easy enough to preach patience, but he had not reckoned with all the contingencies and when he saw the Yard people working in almost intolerable conditions he boiled inwardly. One day he let caution fly and spoke to his father about it.

It was a Saturday evening, dinner was over and he and his father were alone in the dining room when he remarked that the lorries were making life difficult for the traders of Sparrow's Yard and asked if nothing could be done to help them.

Cyril Redmayne was scanning the evening paper and he did not bother to look up. "Can you suggest anything?" he asked off-handedly, "bearing in mind that it's the stalls that are obstructing the lorries."

"You must admit life's difficult for them. They have to make a living and

222

there's nowhere else for them to go," Johnny said.

"That isn't my worry," replied his father, rustling his paper impatiently.

"But they ought to be shown some consideration. After all, it was Grandfather who let them trade there in the first place and it's a bit rotten if you make life impossible for them now," said Johnny, speaking with more heat in his voice than he had intended.

"You seem to know a great deal about it and you obviously can't mind your own business," remarked Cyril. "Perhaps you'll remember I advised you to have nothing to do with the Yard when we first came to live here? I'm repeating that advice now and you'd do well to take it."

He reopened the paper which he had closed while he spoke and resumed reading as though the matter were ended. Johnny's hands were damp and his heart was beating loudly. He wished he knew how to force his father to see the situation as it appeared to him but he knew it was impossible to move him. There he sat, apparently emotionless, his thin grey hair sleeked down to his head, his large well-

kept hands with the immaculately mani-
cured nails holding the newspaper. He
looked at that moment the personification
of power and insolence—he was steely,
ruthless, inhuman, and Johnny found
himself wondering where his vulnerable
point was hidden. What kind of life could
his mother have had? He had never seen
any show of affection between them; their
endearments were formal, their kisses
perfunctory. Was it possible that they
could ever have felt as he and Iris did?

"Dad," he said suddenly, "why are you
so dead set against the whole human race?
My grandfather must have thought a lot of
those people in the Yard or he'd never
have let them work there."

"Now look, Johnny, let's get this
straight," Cyril Redmayne answered.
"Your grandfather didn't give a damn
about what his wife went through. You
think you know everything but there are
some things you don't understand. My
mother couldn't help being revolted by
those people and by all the other scabby
beggars who came to the house. She was
not unkind. It was simply that she couldn't

bear to see, touch or smell them. It was just her nature."

"But they're not repulsive now," Johnny said. "I think they're wonderful. They make people like us seem as tame as goldfish."

"You'll change your tune when you know them better," his father said.

"I don't think so," said Johnny. "But whoever or whatever the Yard people may be I still say you're giving them a rotten deal."

"I don't wish to discuss the matter any further," Cyril said. "Go and play your piano and leave me in peace."

"Not before you listen to what I have to say. I know you're only allowing the stalls to stay in the Yard so long as I don't see Iris. You practically blackmailed Mrs. Crockett."

He paused, but his father went on reading and ignored the outburst.

"Listen, Dad. Iris and I love each other," Johnny went on earnestly. "We're not giving you an excuse to break up the Yard but you won't win."

"Won't I?" said Cyril with a smile.

"No," said Johnny, but he felt small

and ineffectual, and he regretted allowing himself to grow so heated. His father's manner had roused him to say more than he intended and already he feared that he had endangered Iris and her people still further.

As he crossed the hall his mother came out of the drawing room and laid her hand on his arm. She looked anxious as she said: "Were you arguing with your father about the Yard, Johnny? Don't. Don't antagonize him. It isn't wise."

"Well, it's so rotten the way those stall people are being pushed around," he said. "I'd feel the same even if I didn't know them."

"Yes, I know, dear. But this is his concern," Helen Redmayne said.

"I can't stand by and say nothing," Johnny replied, but he was in no mood for music now. He was working on a new song with Reub Hillstein and he needed to concentrate, but as soon as he sat down at his piano his mother came into the room.

"I only want to say you'd much better be careful," she said urgently. "Please don't think I'm against Iris, dear. She's lovely, but quite honestly she's not our sort."

"What is our sort?" he asked. "Our sort seems a bloodless, inhuman sort if Dad's an example. I'd rather belong to the other lot."

"I know you feel strongly now, but this will all die down," she said. "You'll get over Iris."

"No," he said. "This is the real thing."

"Johnny," she said in a pleading tone.

"It's no use. We're serious and we don't care how long we have to wait. We can't get married as things are with all those stallholders at Dad's mercy. But things will change. Tom Crockett will come out of prison, for one thing. Meantime I can't keep quiet when I see Iris's people badly treated."

"Your father has always had a thing about those stall people," his mother said. "Especially the Crocketts. You'd be very stupid to aggravate him."

Johnny turned to the piano uneasily when she left him, but soon he was deep in his work and he lost count of time.

It was wonderful working with Reub and going to Maurice's flat to talk and

227

discuss and argue. He had never expected anyone to take his jingles seriously, far less to encourage him and to suggest projects he would never have thought himself anywhere near good enough to tackle.

Maurice and Reub had listened quietly when he told them his idea of interpreting the Yard in terms of music and he had expected them to dismiss it, but they were both so wildly enthusiastic he could scarcely believe it and now he was trying to translate his ideas into sound.

With his mind full of this project he soon forgot the argument with his father and he did not think about it again until one day about a fortnight later when he was at work.

The day was one like any other till he was summoned to the manager's office. He could think of no reason why he should be called and as he knocked at the door he tried to think if he had been careless over anything. He was soon relieved on that score.

"Well, Redmayne, I've got some good news for you," the manager said genially. He was holding a letter and he glanced over the top of it as he spoke. "The bank has a new scheme to give our young clerks wider experience and the chance to work abroad for a spell. You've worked hard and your report was excellent so I was very pleased to recommend you as a candidate. You are one of the first to be selected for a post."

Johnny felt as though he had been hit over the head but he had enough presence of mind to express his thanks.

"You are to join our Paris office," the manager beamed. "A wonderful opportunity, Redmayne. I suppose this is a complete surprise, eh?"

"Yes," stammered Johnny, standing to attention. "It is rather."

"Well, there's no place like Paris in the spring. You're a very lucky fellow."

Johnny swallowed hard. "How long shall I be there, sir?" he asked, realizing as he spoke that this was not exactly the right question.

"Oh, probably a year or two. It isn't specified," was the reply.

"Thank you, sir," Johnny said, and he stumbled out of the office and down to the washroom feeling dazed and sick.

The news soon spread and the rest of

the day was utterly unreal. Most of his fellow clerks envied him and not so long ago he would have thought anyone lucky to have such a chance. But now! Now there was Iris and he wanted to be near in case she needed him. It was not long to her examination and with life as it was in the Yard he knew that his presence helped her even though he could do so little. He was there and that was what mattered.

Lucky old Redmayne, his fellow clerks said. Yes, he was lucky. For him new scenes, new excitements, he recognized the truth of this; but for Iris there would be the ever-increasing anxiety of Sparrow's Yard and the growing sense of responsibility as the situation worsened.

In his heart Johnny felt certain that his father was at the bottom of this move, he was sure he had pulled strings to bring it about so he was in the mood to throw caution to the wind and he went straight to Lantern Place after work and called at Aunt Camille's. It seemed to him that there could be nothing to lose by going there now.

Iris opened the door and when she saw

him her face lit up. "Has your father thought better of it?" she asked eagerly.

He shook his head and told her the news and its effect on her was as bad as he had feared it would be. She sank down into Ascot's chair because her legs were trembling so. Her hands were clammy and she wiped them on her handkerchief and then rolled it into a ball and gripped it in her fist. Tears streaked her face with mascara and she looked like a waif—a lost, dirty little waif stranded in an alien world.

Looking at her Melia saw aspects of her own self: she saw the Melia who had played in Sparrow's Yard and encountered Cyril Redmayne there, she saw the Melia whose gay young husband had deserted her for another woman, and a great anger was borne in her. For an instant, brief as a flash of lightning, Johnny appeared as an enemy, the son of the man who hated them and would destroy them, and she thought of Tom with longing because she needed the comfort of his physical presence and sheer strength. Inside her mind she called out to him and for a moment she felt a terrible claustrophobia because he was incarcerated in a prison cell and she wanted to run out like a revolutionary, screaming, tearing her hair and creating a great noise from her sorrow.

This mood disappeared almost as soon as it was born. Camille was comforting Iris and encouraging Johnny and by a super-human effort Melia made her voice sound optimistic. Of course this move was a good thing! Think of the things he would see and all he would be able to tell them. Why, if he were in the Army a post to Paris would be a piece of cake!

Johnny stayed the whole evening and he and Iris took leave of each other under the old gas lamp with the light shining on Uncle Harry's cockle shells.

When he had gone she went up to her own room and sat on the edge of the bed. She loved him so desperately and the idea of his absence was so terrible that she had to press her hands over her mouth to stop herself from crying out loud. Where did people get strength and determination and will power from, she wondered. There was none inside her. There was only a beaten, frightened creature inside, a creature that only felt safe when it had someone to cling to and draw strength from, a despicable, cowardly creature.

She went over to the glass, wondering if her own mirrored face would reflect back any help. She saw there the good looks she inherited from her father allied with the determination of her mother's family. Old Ascot, Auntie Camille, Melia—in her face there was a strange, indefinable look of them all. It was not in the features, it was in the expression. "Well," she thought, "they've survived and so shall I. I didn't curl up before when things went wrong and I'm not curling up now. I'll stand up because of Johnny and Ma and Tom and I won't be beaten by you, Cyril Redmayne."

The move had one advantage. For the few days before Johnny went away he came to Lantern Place every evening. Nobody who saw the two of them together at this time doubted that their love was real or treated it as a boy-and-girl affair and the evening before he left for Paris Aunt Camille gave a party for them and, as Ascot said, it was just like Christmas.

They sang all the old songs and a wonderful spirit of optimism began to grow, but Iris knew the next day would be hard.

When would they meet again? Her eyes met Johnny's and she blinked away the threatening tears. He came across the room and took her hand.

"Soon," he said. "We'll meet again soon."

17

THE hardest part of their separation was the uncertainty of its length. Iris was bad at letter writing and though at night, just before she fell asleep, words would come in a limpid flow the same words seemed flat and inadequate when she was confronted with a blank sheet of paper next day. She would only manage a few stilted phrases, digging her pen into the paper as she wrote.

Now that Johnny was out of the country and there was no possibility of seeing him she felt as though she had passed through a shattering experience and was living in a void. The only thing she could look forward to with any certainty was Tom's release and until then the days were just so much time to be got through.

Well, she would just put all her energy into the work at Abbeyfield and when the course was over she would get the best job she could and slave away at improving herself. There were lots of things she could do. Johnny had suggested she should take up French and as soon as the examination was over she meant to. It was no good mooning about the place like a sick cow.

The week after Johnny left she passed her driving test but she continued to go out with Alfie one evening a week to keep her hand in. She felt strained when they were together and wished she could talk to him about Johnny.

Occasionally she caught a fleeting glimpse of Raymond Perks but it was always from a distance. His mother had had her operation and Ascot heard that she was recovering though Mrs. Tilley declared that she had scarcely known her when they passed each other in the street.

"That lilac jersey suit just floats on her," she informed the others. "And those eyes. Wicked!"

"Trust old Tilley to look on the black side," exclaimed Glad Cheek. "I didn't think she looked nearly so bad when I saw her. If she doubled her rations she'd be right in no time. Wants a bit of weight, that's all."

It was almost Easter now and Iris found herself dreading the holiday. She would not be able to go anywhere without missing Johnny and she often found herself searching the faces of the passers-by in the fruitless hope that she might see him.

The Saturday before Easter was one of those grey muggy March days. Iris was serving at the stall in the morning when she saw Florrie Perks on the other side of the Yard looking as though she was out for trouble.

She wore a new, almond-green suit and with her striking natural auburn hair she automatically attracted notice.

After a bit she sauntered across to the Crocketts' stall on her high stiletto heels and spoke to Melia in a loud and insolent tone.

"I'll take a pound of spuds, my good woman," she said.

Melia weighed the potatoes and shot them into Florrie's bag without a word.

"Give me a cauliflower," demanded Florrie. "Not that one, it's all marked, look! Ought to throw it away you did."

Melia replaced the cauliflower which suffered from nothing but a broken floweret and gave Florrie a perfect one.

"That's better. You'll learn in time. I'll take half of tomatoes, and none of your specked ones," Florrie went on. "Here, look at this potato you give me! Sea-green and all eyes!"

"I'll give you all eyes in a minute, Miss Perks," muttered Melia between her teeth.

"What was that you said?" demanded Florrie in a loud tone.

"I asked if there's anything else you want," replied Melia. "There's other customers besides you, my lady."

The two were at the front of the stall, for Florrie had followed Melia to watch her weigh the tomatoes and now they were the centre of an interested group of spectators. Iris was serving as fast as she could but now she called out:

"Customers waiting this side, Ma."

"Coming," replied Melia.

"Oh no, you don't," replied Florrie Perks. "I'll have some service if you don't mind. Just weigh me up a few pot herbs."

"Pot herbs!" echoed Melia. "You're living in the past, aren't you? Iris, throw me a couple of carrots for Miss Perks."

Florrie Perks' face became suffused with an angry purple.

238

"Don't you stand there calling me Miss Perks in front of all these people," she shouted. "I'm the rightful Mrs. Crockett, I'd have you know, and any decent woman would have stood aside and let my poor children have a name the same as what yours has got."

By this time Iris had attracted Uncle Wally's attention and he came round to the rear of the stall unobserved by Florrie.

"'Ere! Be off with you," he shouted, almost in her ear.

Taken unawares, she jumped, backed and stepped straight in the path of an oncoming lorry, which swerved smartly and caught the offside of Mrs. Tilley's stall scattering the carefully piled-up fruit far and wide.

A gasp of horror rose in Sparrow's Yard as apples, oranges, lemons, grapes and bananas hurtled to the ground to be crushed by the lorry wheels so that the broken flagstones resembled the canvas of a surrealist artist. It was an abstract of brilliance and horror.

Melia and Wally both stood staring aghast at what had happened and the lorry driver jumped down from his cab swearing death and worse to the person who had caused the accident. Mrs. Tilley still sat on her wooden box, her face frozen into an expression of uncomprehending surprise which gradually gave way to one of fury.

"Keep serving," Melia said to Iris. "I'm going over to help Mrs. Tilley."

Alfie and Wally righted the stall and Melia took a broom and began to sweep the ruined fruit into a heap while the Cheek girls came and gathered up as much of the sound fruit as they could. Mrs. Tilley still sat on the box blinking her bewildered eyes and uttering angry but unintelligible noises.

"It's the shock, and no wonder," said Winnie Cheek. "I'd like to see that Florrie Perks turned to raspberry jam, I would."

Melia bit her lip. "I'd have thought we had enough trouble with all these lorries busting up our trade," she said bitterly. "It's more them than her, if you ask me."

Mrs. Tilley suddenly came back to earth. "It's high time us people did something about this," she declared. "I reckon we ought to complain."

"Who to?" asked Melia.

"Ah. That's just it."

"Reckon we'll close down early today, Mum," Alfie said. "We were doing well, too," said Mrs. Tilley. "Who's to make good all that on the ground, I'd like to know?"

While they worked to put the stall to rights Iris had her hands full on the other side of the Yard. Some of the customers had seen Florrie Perks before and they could not resist conjecturing and asking questions.

"She a relation of yours, duck? Aunt or something?" one of them asked.

"Not that I know," said Iris briefly.

"Proper trouble-maker, eh?" said another.

"Poor thing seems to have a grievance," said another, with a loud sniff.

Iris ignored them all and refused to be drawn, but her mind felt like a whirlpool. Somehow the trouble Florrie Perks always managed to cause was worse than the changes in the Yard. These latter were brought about by forces they could not control and, like tempest and flood, they had to be accepted, but Florrie was one of their own kind and she was evil.

Iris knew all about the way she had

stolen her father from Ma and Tom and kept him for many long years to their shame and distress. She hated her. The very thought of the woman filled her with loathing and made her pitch the potatoes angrily into the scales and give overweight just like Ascot did. But for the havoc Florrie had wrought in the family Tom might well have been a different character.

"Bramleys? Yes, they're in their prime."

No wonder Tom had resented it when Dad came back, but wasn't it funny how he loved him, all fierce and angry and pent-up and doing things he shouldn't like running away?

"And one of carrots, did you say?"

Of course he saw what Ma went through standing at the stall every day with Gran! That's why he had said he would make it all up to her and give her a full-length fur coat so she could look as grand as Florrie Perks—grander. No wonder he couldn't wait to earn it.

"All right. I'm sorry. I never heard you ask for the onions."

Maybe it would have been better if Dad had never come back—they were rubbing along all right, Gran and Ma and Tom. Only then there wouldn't have been me. Perhaps it would have been better if there hadn't been me!

"Six of whites? That's right—you hold the bag open—we'll manage."

I bet it made Tom feel out of it seeing me there in the cradle! There now, I'm getting myself all worked up. Oh my God, that Florrie Perks! Women like her ought to be skinned alive and not let loose to break up other people's homes. Ma, oh Ma, I wish I could make it up to you. It's so hard not to cry!

She turned her back to the stall and blew her nose loudly. When she turned back, blinking the tears out of her eyes, she saw that the lorry had moved off, and Florrie Perks, who had managed to get herself lost in the crowd, was momentarily isolated in the middle of the Yard. Mrs. Tilley saw this too and as though she had suddenly been galvanized into action she leapt from her box with surprising agility and approached Florrie, thrusting her large face forward.

"See what you done?" she bellowed. "Upset all my fruit! It was you, not the lorry, done that, Florrie Perks, and I hope you're satisfied."

The two women immediately became the centre of attention and a crowd gathered round them.

"Go on, then. What've you got to say?" demanded Mrs. Tilley. "It ain't like you to keep quiet, Miss Perks. Coming here disturbing the peace!"

"Come on, Mum. Come on home!" Raymond Perks had thrust his way through the crowd and he took his mother's arm. "Come on," he said again. "It won't do you no good staying here."

Florrie looked up at him and then she looked at the pile of ruined fruit and last of all she looked at Mrs. Tilley. Everyone waited for her to retort in her usual way with a jibe or an insult, but her lip trembled and an ugly, noisy, gobbling sob broke from her. Raymond put his arm round her shoulders. "Come on home, old dear," he said.

He led her away without protest and the Yard people gazed at one another in amazement.

"Well, whatever's come over Florrie?" they asked.

They were still recovering from the shock of seeing her subdued when Cyril Redmayne drove into the Yard. The crowd was slow to disperse and he was forced to come to a halt by the fruit stall, where Mrs. Tilley was explaining the cause of the commotion to some people who had arrived too late to witness it. Suddenly she saw Mr. Redmayne and their eyes met. Without any warning she advanced on the car and the spectators saw that she meant to tell him exactly what she thought of conditions in the Yard. She, who had said that the sight of this man would freeze the words on her lips, was now treating him to a vivid description of what had happened and she was not pulling her punches.

They all expected him to drive on and leave her talking, but when she paused for breath he got out of the car and surveyed the damage.

"Are you insured against this sort of thing?" he asked.

"Insured? Me? With all I've got on my plate? I've got a sick husband what'll never work again. What time do you think *I* get up in the morning?"

"Just a moment. Take it easy," he said, and he pulled out his wallet, extracted some notes and put them in her hand.

"Does that cover it?" he asked.

"Oh!" she exclaimed. "More than."

Before she could recover from her surprise and begin to thank him he had got back in his car and driven off.

"Well!" exclaimed Mrs. Tilley as a slow smile spread across her face. "What do you think of that, eh?"

She held the notes like a fan and waved them above her head.

"See that, Melia?" she called. "Handsome. Real handsome."

Melia had a lump in her throat and she had to fight to keep her emotions under control. It was no use giving way to them, but she wanted to run away from the sight of Mrs. Tilley's triumphant face, for it was almost more than she could stomach. But this was their living and she had got to earn it. Somehow she had to get through the rest of the day.

She felt ugly and squalid in her rough working clothes and when she looked at Iris her heart swelled with indignation and pity. The girl looked almost plain with her bright hair hidden under a scarf and her lips set in a hard line. She was serving badly, too. She was getting flustered and not giving the kind of attention that Melia liked to see.

"Here, dearie, you go off home for a bit," she said. "You look tired out. Go and sit with Ascot—she'll cheer you up."

For once Iris did not argue.

"All right, Ma," she said.

But the events of that morning upset her so much that she could not forget them and Camille tried to think of ways to take her out of herself. On Sunday evening when Maurice was with them she suggested they should have a change at Easter. "What about a trip to Windsor or Hampton Court?" she said.

"What about my little place for a change?" asked Maurice.

"I wasn't joking, Maurice," said Camille sternly.

"Neither was I. It'd be a good idea if Iris came down to my farmhouse for a few days. You wouldn't mind I suppose, would you, Melia?"

"Me mind? I'd say it would do the girl all the good in the world," replied Melia gratefully. "That's very thoughtful of you, Maurice."

"How about it, Iris?" he asked her.

Iris's face had grown bright with excitement.

"Oh, how wonderful. France!" she exclaimed.

"It's nowhere near Paris," Maurice reminded her.

"Never mind that. Johnny and I will be on the same continent again. But what about the stall over Easter, Ma? It's always so busy."

"You forget the stall for once and enjoy yourself," said Melia.

"The change will just set you up nicely for the exam," remarked Camille.

"Set you up, too," said Maurice. "You're coming with us, Camel. You can't let a young man like me go about without a chaperone."

"Me?" echoed Camille. "Don't talk so silly, Maurice. How can I come? There's Harry's supper to see to and the midday meals for Melia and Wally——"

"And what's wrong with me taking over that lot?" interrupted Ascot. "Nobody's bothered to speak to me for the last half-hour and I'm about tired of being treated like a cracked pint pot. You just leave things to me, young Camel. You're not so clever we can't do without you sometimes."

"Good old Ascot, give it to 'em straight, old gal!" shouted Wally. "I just fancy a bit of your cooking for a change."

"You hear what Wally says?" crowed Ascot proudly.

"Well, all right, then," Camille agreed, "but there's no call to be so nasty about it, and don't forget Harry likes a nice cup of tea when he gets in from the theatre."

"That's right," agreed Harry, who had listened to all this without a word. He knew from experience that Camille would never take a holiday away from them all until she was practically insulted into doing so.

So on Maundy Thursday Maurice, Camille and Iris flew down to Nice, where a car was waiting to meet them. Maurice had been looking very pleased with himself all the way in the plane and every now and then he had chuckled over some private joke which he refused to share.

After they left the airport he drove them

some way along the coast road so that they could catch their first breath-taking glimpse of the bay and Camille's face was a study of mingled pleasure and regret when she saw the almost unbelievable beauty of it.

"Whatever would Melia say to this?" she cried. "Oh, how I wish Harry were here! Oh my word, there's nothing you can say, is there, Iris? Those colours!"

"You can't really believe it's always here, can you?" Iris said. "Does it vanish when you look the other way?"

She felt the warmth of the sun on her arms and face and the thought of Tom came into her mind. One day, when everything was all right, perhaps they would all come here together: she and Johnny and Tom and Ma and all of them. The idea filled her with a joy that was not far removed from sadness because it was as though they had already shared the wonder of it and now it had gone into that strange past where things which have only been wished preserve a peculiar reality.

Maurice was humming a tune to himself. "Seen enough? Shall we make for home?" he asked.

Neither of them had seen nearly enough, but they agreed it was time to go, and presently Maurice struck inland along the road through Grasse, where acre upon acre of hyacinths and narcissi filled the air with their scent. Iris had never been further from home than the seaside resorts near London and the vastness of Provence, the limitless stretches of field and mountain and the occasional brilliant blue flash of water in a mountain pool, dazzled her.

At last Maurice brought the car to a halt on a mountain road beneath which mile upon mile of open country stretched into a blue distance.

"Here we are," he said.

"But where's the house?" asked Camille.

Maurice chuckled. "Just down that little hill," he replied, and they turned into a lane that was almost concealed by a grassy bank thick with spring flowers. They passed a few cottages and then stopped before a low, stone-built house which seemed almost to grow out of the hillside.

"Why, Maurice, this really is away from it all!" exclaimed Camille.

Iris was breathing in the wonderful,

sweet-smelling air and trying to distinguish the mingled scents. She closed her eyes and opened them again. She had never dreamed of anything so beautiful.

"Let's go in," Maurice said.

The door opened straight into a large room with a polished tiled floor. It was rather dark, but Iris could make out some pictures on the walls and a large open stone fireplace. As they entered an elderly woman wearing an apron over her black dress came hurrying to meet them and she greeted Maurice volubly and delightedly. Camille did not understand any of it and Iris only caught a word here and there, but this did not deter the little woman and she rattled on to both of them as enthusiastically as she had to Maurice and as though their lack of comprehension did not matter in the least.

"Marie Claire will show you up," Maurice said, "and I'll just take a peek in the kitchen to see what she's cooking for us."

Whatever was cooking smelt delicious and Iris and Aunt Camille exchanged appreciative glances as they followed Marie Claire up a shallow staircase to the room they were to share. She crossed to the window and pushed the shutters open indicating the immensity of the view before them with a wide sweep of her arms as though it was hers but she was willing to share it.

"Wouldn't it be wonderful if the whole family were here?" remarked Iris, when they were alone.

"Not really, dear," replied Camille in a matter-of-fact voice. "I expect we'd all be quarrelling and you may be sure Uncle Wally would hate the cooking. Come on, let's hurry up and go down."

"Lucky we didn't bring much to unpack," Iris said. "I shall stay as I am."

The drive in Maurice's open car had given her a slight tan and Camille thought she had never seen her look so beautiful. She really is beautiful, her aunt thought, screwing up her eyes and peering at her own reflection in the glass. She took off her heavily trimmed hat, tidied her hair and said: "Well, that's better. I can hear Maurice at the piano already. I do hope they'll give us a nice cup of tea, Iris, I'm dying for one."

"I expect they will," Iris said, and they

went down the shallow staircase which had a single turn and then led straight into the room they had entered when they arrived.

Now that she was accustomed to the light Iris saw there was a grand piano in the far corner. Someone was playing it but it was not Maurice for he was standing beside it beating time and a young man she had never seen before was sitting on the window seat. Suddenly she turned and caught Camille's hand.

"Oh, Auntie!" she gasped, and she sped down the remaining stairs and across the room.

"Johnny!" she cried, and she was whirled off her feet and clasped close by the man who had been playing the piano.

For a moment they were completely lost in the ecstasy of their reunion; then came the exclamations, questions, bewilderment and delight. While Maurice tried to explain, and was constantly interrupted, the dark-haired young man watched them with a benevolent air as though they were all children and he was very, very old.

Suddenly Maurice noticed him and began to apologize. "Why, Reub!" he exclaimed, "come and meet my old friend

Camel, and young Iris here. Camel, old dear, this is Reub Hillstein. He's down here for a little bit of peace to get on with some work."

"Why, bless my soul, you're one of the people I've always wanted to meet!" exclaimed Camille. "You've been a name in our house ever since *The Silver Staircase*."

Reub, Camille and Maurice immediately entered into a conversation on their favourite topic and before long Reub was listening to Camille's tales of the music halls of thirty years ago with a special interest.

"Now then," admonished Maurice, as Marie Claire brought in a tea tray which she set before Camille, "don't go letting Camel carry you away, Reub. You've other fish to fry first, remember."

"I'm not forgetting," said Reub. "This is just something for the store. Another little seed."

"You want to be careful—you might get a few weeds thrown in, my boy," Maurice said.

"Now then young Maurice, I don't want any of your disrespect," said Camille.

"And how's that young Johnny getting on? Keeping you busy at the bank, dear?"

"Too busy," he said.

"Written any more nice songs?"

"I'm keeping at them," Johnny said. "Maybe one or two will get by. It's made all the difference having Reub to work with."

Camille's bright little eyes sparkled at this, but she managed to smother an exclamation. If Reub Hillstein were really working with Johnny who could tell what might happen? She sipped her tea and found it more exhilarating than champagne. This was wonderful. It was a tonic she had never expected and she felt as though she had shed twenty years and was right back in her own natural element.

Iris had not said very much. She was sitting beside Johnny on the piano stool, looking so happy that Camille wished she could take a snapshot of her.

Presently Maurice said: "Why don't you two kids go out for a walk and get up an appetite for dinner? You'll have to do it justice or Marie Claire will be offended and she's putting on a very special effort."

As Johnny and Iris went out through the

enormous kitchen succulent smells greeted their noses and Marie Claire's little red face creased up with smiles. She said a lot of things which made Johnny laugh.

"What on earth was she talking about?" Iris asked as soon as they were outside.

"Just predicting that we shall have extremely beautiful children," Johnny said. "We shall, too."

"Of course we shall," Iris said. "Come on, let's go and sit over there on the bank. I want to hear everything that's happened."

She had imagined they would never stop talking, but it did not take them long to exchange their news. But the joy of being together again made a fool of time and an hour passed more swiftly than one long minute when they were separated.

"Tell me about Reub," she said at last. "What's he doing here? You kept very quiet about him in your letters."

"I had a few ideas that Maurice knew about and he thought Reub might be able to help and by golly he can. It's only tentative you know, sort of exploring the way, but being able to talk about it is so absolutely grand. It's something I've always dreamed about but never done. Even if nothing comes of my ideas it will have been a wonderful experience."

"Something will come of them," she said, "but I can't believe anything could better 'The Old Songs'. I shall never love anything so much."

"That's because it's our special; it came with that first sight of Sparrow's Yard, remember?"

"I'm not likely to forget," she said. "Isn't this heaven, Johnny? I bet there must be thousands of people who never get as much of heaven as this, not all their lives through."

"Millions," he said. "Let's make the most of it."

The dusk was beginning to fall, the outlines of the hills were disappearing and the sky was streaked with red. They felt as though they were alone in the immensity of the beauty all round them. Iris had never known quietness and it overwhelmed her. She almost doubted that she was the Iris of Lantern Place and the wonder of this reunion which had come like a gift, completed the illusion.

But there was no illusion about the

dinner that evening and Maurice had not exaggerated Marie Claire's culinary powers. They sat down to a meal which was superb in every detail and they did full justice to every course. Afterwards they sat and listened to Maurice playing and singing but as they were all tired no one was inclined to stay up late.

Maurice stayed on at the piano after they had said good night. He hoped this thing between Reub and Johnny would work out and he believed it would but he was not going to bank on it yet or encourage anybody else to. Somehow he felt lonely, even more lonely because of the young people in the house. He loved having them but although they would never have guessed it it was a bitter-sweet enjoyment for him because they put him in mind of himself and Milly.

He began to play Chopin, which was something nobody ever heard him do. He played a nocturne and had no idea that Camille, hearing the sound, had crept out of her room and halfway down the stairs. She only stayed for a second, but the glimpse of Maurice's stocky figure and his head bent over the keys touched her heart.

She was the only other person who had
known Milly and she would not have
intruded on his special music for her for
the world.

18

THE Easter holiday went by far too quickly, but to Iris and Johnny it was an interlude of such happiness that they had to keep reminding themselves they were not dreaming. They had never been able to spend such long stretches of time together, they had never been under the same roof all night and at table together for their meals. And such meals!

"Don't forget this is a working holiday," Maurice reminded them, and in the afternoons he whisked Iris and Camille out in the car so that Johnny and Reub were left undisturbed.

"I can do with one or two good numbers," he remarked.

"And do you really believe Johnny will turn them out?" Iris asked.

"Take a look at me, girl," Maurice ordered. "I'm not a softie who's helping a maybe. My head's about as hard as that rock over there. If I don't discover young

Johnny then someone else will, but someone else might take a lot longer about it. Now he's met Reub he's got a wonderful chance."

"Hard head or not, Maurice, next to Johnny and the family I love you best in all the world," she said, and she hugged him and rubbed her cheek against his. "Thank you for giving us this wonderful time," she said, "and thank you for Reub. Thank you especially for him."

It was Johnny who drove Iris and Aunt Camille to the airport at Nice on the Tuesday after Easter. He still had another day's leave and Maurice and Reub were going back with him to spend a few days in Paris before they came home.

"When shall we all meet again?" Iris asked, depressed by the thought that soon the sea would be between them again.

"Sooner than we expect, perhaps," said Johnny. "After all, we didn't expect this, did we?"

Aunt Camille had gone to make a completely unnecessary enquiry so that they might be by themselves for as long as possible but now their flight was called and the time had come.

Johnny hugged Aunt Camille and he and Iris exchanged their last kiss.

"See you soon," they all said.

The plane took off in brilliant sunshine and landed in drenching rain. It was cold and drear and Iris and Camille agreed they must have imagined that wonderful bay and the road to Maurice's farmhouse and all the smells and the wild flowers and even Marie Claire.

"I don't think we imagined the food though," Camille remarked. "I'm sure I've put on pounds. And you look so well, Iris, that Ma won't know you."

The family at Lantern Place sat up late that night listening to the account of the holiday. At home the weekend had been uneventful and there had been no trouble in the Yard. Since the fracas with Florrie Perks the lorries had driven at snail's pace so as not to disturb the stallholders and the Tilleys and the Cheeks were actually growing optimistic about the future now. They could not speak too highly of Cyril Redmayne. They said they were sure to find themselves in clover when the offices were finished and the Yard was paved over all nice and tidy. Their smugness irked

Melia sorely, for she thought of the price she and Iris were paying for their peace and sometimes she hinted tartly that she had a good mind to give up and get a job in a shop.

"That may be all right for you," Mrs. Tilley said, "but I certainly shan't move. I've got to think of Ernie, and Alfie and I can take turn and turn about at the stall."

"That's just it," Melia thought bitterly. "You've got Ernie and I've got Tom. We've all got someone. I wish I could go to Australia. Anywhere. Just to be on my own for once."

But now the news of the holiday cheered her almost as much as though she had been away herself and she began to share the optimistic mood Iris and Camille had brought home.

It was six weeks now till the examination and Iris went back to the Technical College feeling far better able to face it than she had done before Easter.

"You look as though you've been on the Riviera," Caroline said, when she remarked how well Iris looked.

"So I have," said Iris. "At least, I saw it. Aunt Camille and I went to stay with

Maurice Royal at his place just near Grasse."

"Iris! Not *the* Maurice Royal? Ooh, you never said you knew him even."

"I've known him ever since I was born," said Iris. "He's been a friend of the family for centuries."

"I can't wait to tell Mother," Caroline said. "He's her pin-up boy. What's he like to know?"

"Just fab," Iris said.

"Well, I'm glad you enjoyed yourself," said Caroline in a tone of relief, for she had been unhappy since she had unwittingly upset Iris with her remarks about the people of Sparrow's Yard.

Iris, too, was glad that their friendly relationship was restored but she could not help reflecting on her new-found confidence. At one time she would never have told anyone about Maurice, yet nothing had really changed. "Except my mood," she thought. "Perhaps other people's moods will change, too."

But when she arrived home that evening she found the family plunged in despair because Uncle Wally had been told that

Dook's stable and their storage shed were to be pulled down at the end of the month.

The formal letter giving him notice had arrived that morning and when Wally read it his face had turned as grey as the stubble on his chin, Ascot said. She had had to make him drink an eggcup full of brandy and he was so stunned that he had not been able to speak until midday.

He was only aware of a weight like a stone inside and of a dreadful hollering in his head like an anguished voice yelling "Aw—aw—aw——" continuously. He did not realize that it meant never more, never more, and that it was his dirge for Dook and all Dook meant to him.

"What's to happen now?" Iris asked, for without Dook they had no transport from market and everybody knew that there was not another stable in the whole of Villa Park.

"This had to come, Wally," Ascot said sadly. "Dook's old. I've often thought it high time he was pensioned off. 'Tisn't fair to have him on the roads no more—not with the traffic like it is today."

"Dook don't mind the traffic all the time I'm with him," Wally said miserably.

"The Tilleys have offered to help out with their van," Melia said. "It's good of them, but we like our independence."

"Why can't we have our own van?" Iris asked.

"Because Tom's not here to drive it," Melia said sharply. "You know that as well as I do."

Iris did not say any more. At last she was confronted with a problem she knew she could solve. With the excuse that she had to study she went up to her own room to think. There was no need to study any more because she was not going to take the examination. She felt curiously flat. It was like rounding a corner expecting to see a view and finding a blank wall.

Tomorrow she would tell Mrs. Drew she was going to leave the college and when that bridge was burnt she would tell Ma. Alfie would help them to choose a van and then she would go to work in the Yard instead of in a fashion house. It was rather an anticlimax, but she did not have to weigh up the pros and cons because there was no other course to take.

Melia went to the pub later that evening. For her the days in the Yard were already over and from the bar she could see Mrs. Tilley, Princess Potter and Winnie and Glad Cheek at their usual table. They were obviously discussing the blow that had fallen on the Crocketts and the Taggs. She took her glass of stout and joined them.

"Alf's more than ready to help you, Melia," Mrs. Tilley said, as she had done many times before.

"It's very kind of him and we appreciate it, but you know how it is. We do like to stand on our own feet," Melia said.

"Ah, I know how you feel about that," said Ernie Tilley, who was raising a half-pint glass in his big clumsy hands. Some of the beer slopped over onto his jacket and Alfie immediately wiped it off. Ernie took a long pull at the beer and said again, "I know how you feel about that, Melia girl."

"Seems to me Mr. Redmayne's not playing fair, pulling down the stable," Alfie said. "He must know a pitch in the Yard's no good to you without a horse."

"That's neither here nor there to him," Melia replied bitterly. "He's not gone back on his promise that we can stay, so it's all right for the rest of you and that's where he's got his pull."

"What do you mean by that, Melia?" demanded Princess Potter. "You sound as though there's something behind all this. Hadn't you better tell us what it is?"

Melia hesitated and then said, "He made his own terms, but they were strictly between him and me."

"I reckon you ought to have told us there were strings attached," said Winnie Cheek. "He treated Tilley handsome when her stall was turned over, you can't deny it. I reckon you ought to go and have an up-and-downer with him. Talk to him straight, same as Tilley did."

"That's right. Let him see you're not afraid," said Mrs. Tilley.

"Perhaps it's time you knew the sort he is to deal with," Melia was stung to reply. "I'll be glad to get it off my chest, but it won't make any difference to the rest of you. There's no call for any of you to be affected by it," and she told them the whole story of Cyril Redmayne's bargain and of Iris and Johnny.

Knowing the depth of Alfie's affection for Iris she could not help feeling mean and treacherous as she spoke and she saw how he gripped his tankard as he listened. She did not expect any of them to approve of the romance between Iris and Cyril Redmayne's son but now she had begun she had to tell them everything.

"You've always been a friend to us, Alfie, and to my Iris," she said to him quietly when she had finished.

"Still am," he said gruffly. "Always will be."

Mrs. Tilley had been sitting very straight and, apart from a frown, her expression was absolutely blank. Then suddenly she lifted her glass and drank down half a pint of stout at a breath. She planted the glass back on the table, glared round at the assembled company and said in a belligerent tone:

"Well, I don't know what you lot are going to do, but the Tilleys are not staying in Sparrow's Yard after that! We're clearing out, Alfie, and we're letting everyone know why."

"Where to?" asked Alfie.

"I don't know yet. All I know is we're not staying there. I only wish you'd told us the truth sooner, Melia Crockett. Why, it makes me curl up to think we've pitched our stalls on that man's land! And I took his money!"

"I'm with you, Tilley," said Princess Potter. "I'm with you all the way."

"Blessed if we shall stop there, then," declared Winnie Cheek. "If Glad and I can't get another pitch we'll go out office cleaning."

"Seems we're all agreed, then," said Mrs. Tilley grandly. "The stallholders of Sparrow's Yard are about to seek other quarters," and rising from her seat she wheeled Ernie out of the pub with the air of an actress leaving the stage to a round of applause.

"It's very brave of your mum to take that line," Melia told Alfie, "but I shan't think any the less of her if she's changed her tune by morning. I appreciate her sentiments."

"Tilley speaks for all of us," said Princess Potter, and she announced that she was ready to approach shopkeepers, banks and pubs for permission to sell from a basket outside their premises.

Melia felt comforted when she got up to go and she was further cheered by the landlord, who beckoned her to the bar and commiserated with her over their misfortune.

"I can't offer Dook a stable, but old Wally can keep his fish stall in our back-yard if that's any help," he said. "At least it'd be something for him Saturday nights."

"That's real kind of you," Melia answered gratefully. "It'll be something to occupy his mind. Poor old Wally's going to be lost without Dook."

The news of Wally Tagg's calamity spread fast and when the local paper came out later in the week it carried an article about the changes in Sparrow's Yard illustrated by some of Bill Ramsay's photographs.

Next evening a national paper took up the story and featured it with the same photographs, but by that time the family in Lantern Place had other things to think about, for Iris had told them she was going to leave college and help them to keep the business going till Tom came out of prison. She had the whole thing worked out.

When Melia heard what Iris proposed

she was taken too much by surprise to protest forcibly at first but at Abbeyfield Mrs. Drew did her utmost to persuade her to finish the course. She found it impossible to sway her although Iris did agree to stay until she actually possessed the van. Mrs. Drew also helped the family in a way that relieved them of some of the worst of their anxiety by finding a home for Dook. She had a brother who farmed fifty miles from Villa Park and when he heard the story he offered to take the old horse and care for him for the rest of his life.

This news was a tonic to them all for the thought of Dook being put down had dwarfed their other worries.

"Seems like this is the answer, then," said Ascot. "It's worth a fortune. Not too far from home either. You'll be able to go down to see him Sundays, Wally."

"How am I to live day by day, though?" Wally groaned. "I know Dook and he knows me. There's no speaking person like him."

"Still, think how good for him. Lovely green fields and all," Melia said. "I shall be able to tell Tom. He'll like to think of Dook in the country."

Melia knew that news of the events in Sparrow's Yard must have reached her son and she feared his reaction. The story had featured in several daily papers and although the accent was always on the need for progress there was a decided note of regret because something picturesque from the past was going and without mentioning the name of Redmayne the stories were slanted skilfully against him.

Cyril Redmayne himself was only too well aware of this. He hated publicity and had always managed to avoid it, but now he felt that it was only a matter of time before his name was mentioned in connection with the Sparrow's Yard affair and the latest news of the Yard told the story in a series of photographs.

There was a sentimental one of Dook surrounded by a group of admiring children and there was one of Wally outside the empty stable. The pictured eyes of Dr. Redmayne on one side of the page appeared to look gently in the direction of his son, shown as a hard faced tycoon on the other. The last photograph of all had been taken that day and it showed Dook being coaxed to enter a horse box for his journey to the green fields and his retirement.

Cyril tossed the paper angrily aside and went home. He was not looking forward to his evening because Helen had been in a restless mood ever since Johnny had gone to Paris and she had next to nothing to say to him. When he went in she was watching television and she scarcely bothered to look up.

"Dinner will be at eight," she said.

He dropped a token kiss on the top of her head and sat down in the opposite chair. He did not enjoy television and would have liked to turn it off, but she was absorbed and presently he began to watch, too, and became interested against his will.

She was watching one of the daily magazine programmes full of items of general interest and Cyril could not help admiring the skill of the interviewers and the cunning way with which they posed their questions.

"Damn' sauce those fellows have got," he muttered. "I don't know why people answer their silly questions."

"Ssh. Look!" exclaimed Helen sharply.

He looked and clutched the arms of his chair. The camera was tracking along their own High Road and it stopped at Sparrow's Yard. There it was. There were the stalls and their owners just as they appeared every day. There was the hoarding in the background and the rising walls of the Redmayne building.

The camera surveyed the scene and the practised voice of one of the best-known broadcasters began to tell the story of Sparrow's Yard in his own compelling yet deceptively simple style.

Slowly the camera moved up to Princess Potter at her flower stall and she answered the interviewer's questions readily and it seemed as though they were all angled to bring her the full sympathy of the viewer. Then the Tilleys had their turn and after that the camera tracked straight across the Yard to the stall of Amelia Arethusa Crockett.

"I believe you've been in Sparrow's Yard all your life, Mrs. Crockett?" began the interviewer.

"All my life, sir. My mother and father were here before me and Mother still helps of a Saturday when we're hard pushed."

276

"She must be a very old lady now?"

"Getting on for eighty. She was the first one old Dr. Redmayne helped by letting her pitch a stall here."

"Indeed. Are there any others of your family here?"

"Uncle Wally—that's him by the stable —he's the one I rely on most."

"May I have a word with you, sir?"

The camera left Melia and brought Uncle Wally into close-up and Cyril Redmayne saw that the whole script had been planned to lead up to the predicament of the family which had been robbed of transport because the stable was condemned.

"But is there any reason why the stable should be pulled down *now*?" asked the broadcaster.

"Not as I can see. They say it'll be eighteen munfs before the building's finished."

"But this means that you and Mrs. Crockett will have no means of bringing your goods from market, doesn't it?"

"That's the measure of it, sir."

"Do the planners realize this?"

"Must do if they've got anything to think with."

The interview continued, and ended with the broadcaster assuming his well-known expression of sympathetic bewilderment as Mrs. Tilley joined the group and said that all the stallholders hoped to find other pitches.

"We're not staying here after what's happened," she said emphatically.

"But what *has* happened, apart from the business of the stable?" enquired the broadcaster. "Or maybe there's more to it than that?"

Mrs. Tilley pursed her lips and her face loomed large as she slowly shook her head. At this the broadcaster began to wind up in his usual non-committal but pointed way.

"Well, there it is. The story of Sparrow's Yard. A benevolent old doctor —a handful of humble, hard-working stallholders. A stable to be pulled down—for what? For nothing? Your guess is as good as mine."

Helen Redmayne rose and turned off the set; then she switched on the top light. Cyril blinked.

"You've had what I should call a remarkably bad press," she said in a level voice.

"You speak as though I'm the only man who ever wanted to develop his own property," he said. "How do you think plans can go ahead before the ground's cleared? What's to prevent the Crocketts from making other arrangements? The other stallholders don't keep horses and carts."

"I just want you to know one thing," she said. "I hope Johnny will marry Iris and I hope they'll be happy. I know what a lonely marriage is like only too well and I'm not raising a finger to help you prevent him from marrying her if he loves her— and I'm sure he does."

"What do you expect me to do?" he asked sarcastically. "Give them my blessing?"

"Not with that look on your face," she said, and she went out of the room leaving him to his own reflections.

He crossed to the mirror over the fireplace. What was so wrong with his face? What was wrong with him? Helen talked of loneliness as though she had the monopoly of it, but he had never known

279

anything else. His whole life had been an aching emptiness from the days of his miserable childhood till now. He had tried to fill it with success, but success drained away as fast as he poured it in. And whose fault was that, after all? Could he help being as he was? Could he help it if he shared his mother's revulsion from the dirty, smelly humanity at her door? Could he help shrinking from his father's abounding charity which demanded the acceptance of the Yard people as his brethren? These were the questions he asked himself and he could not answer them.

Neither could he meet Helen's eyes as he sat opposite her at their silent dinner table that night.

19

DOOK had gone and without him their business in the Yard was at a standstill. They just had the stock of root vegetables to sell off.

It was Friday and Melia was visiting Tom, so Iris came home from Abbeyfield by way of the Yard. She wanted to know how Alfie's negotiations for the van were going on and when she arrived he was tying the tarpaulin over his mother's stall.

"Seen what you want today, Iris," he said as soon as he saw her. "A van pretty much like ours. I was coming round to see your Ma about it tonight. Price is reasonable."

"We've got to make her buy it, then," Iris said. "I don't see why we shouldn't work up a round, do you?"

"It'll be awful hard work for a girl."

"I'm tough, Alfie! Besides, if Ma can stand out here all day and lug all that stuff about I'm sure I could sell door-to-door from a van. I'd have a good try, anyway. Please, don't *you* try to put me off."

"All right," he said, and they discussed her project at length and he promised her all the help he could give but, like all the others, he still tried to dissuade her from leaving Abbeyfield before she finished her course.

"With your exam only a few weeks off," he said. "I can bring your stuff from market till then. Once you're through college it'll be a different story."

"You know how independent Ma is," explained Iris.

"She can pocket her pride for once, can't she?" he asked. "Want a lift home in the van?"

She clambered in beside him and he put his hand over hers for an instant and swallowed hard. He wore a shabby cravat which had worked loose and she could see the movement of his Adam's apple and the sight of his pale, bare neck touched her so that she wanted to weep.

"All this trouble—it's all because of me!" she cried. "You're all leaving here because of me and Johnny."

"No, duck. It'd only have been a matter

of time before Redmayne threw us out," he said. "Anyway, he's done himself in the eye now. You and Johnny can get married just as soon as you like. Hadn't you thought of that?"

"No," she said. "With Dook going and everything so topsy-turvy I hadn't thought of it at all."

"Well, maybe it's time you did," he said, looking straight in front of him.

"Oh, Alfie, I don't know how ever I'm going to thank you for everything," she said softly.

"Don't try. We'll always understand each other, you and me," he said. With that he pushed his cap back jauntily, revved up and they were away.

Melia was in the sitting room when Iris reached home. She still had on her hat and coat, but she had taken off her shoes and she looked tired and worried.

"Iris, you'll have to drop that idea of leaving Abbeyfield," she said abruptly. "Tom's in a terrible state about it and threatening to break out. He nearly drove me out of my mind this afternoon." She sat down heavily. "That'd be about the last straw," she said. "If he does that it'll finish me and he will if you throw up that course. Here, make me a cup of tea—I'm just about all in."

Iris scurried into the kitchen to put on the kettle and while it was coming to the boil she realized that this would not be an auspicious moment to mention that Alfie had found them a van. Perhaps she could tell her mother about this renewed offer of help instead.

She had just made the tea when there was a knock at the door and she was astounded to find Raymond Perks on the step. She had never told Melia about her meeting with him in the café and now she just stared at him and he stared back. He looked very pale and his brilliant blue eyes were dull and there were dark rings under them.

"Could your Mum come, please?" he said.

"Come where?" asked Iris.

"My mother wants to see her. Please. It's urgent."

Melia was at the sitting-room door now. "What does your mother want with me?" she asked sharply.

"She wants to see you. Please, missis.

She's very ill. They're coming to fetch her back to hospital tonight." Raymond contorted the end of his handsome nose in a sniff and his mouth began to work tremulously.

"Will you come?" he asked.

"Right," Melia said, for she saw that this was not an idle request. "You go on home. I'll be there in ten minutes."

Iris closed the door and Melia began forcing her feet into her shoes.

"I'd better wear my old ones," she said. "Whatever can have got into that Florrie sending for me?"

"He did look bad," said Iris. "He looked as though he'd been crying."

"Oh dear, if only I'd had time for that tea," Melia sighed. "Here, do me shoes up for me, duck. I'm too tired to bend."

She hurried off and Iris was left to drink the stewed tea alone.

Iris had been hoping for a letter from Johnny and she thought it odd that he had not written for several days now. Ma had advised her not to tell him of their predicament because there was nothing he could do to help, but witholding the news had made her letters to him even more stilted than usual, she thought.

She could not stay in the house alone. Aunt Camille would be next door and probably Gran would be with her and she decided to call on them in the hope of raising her spirits.

It had been a warm spring and a huge old lilac tree drooped over the wall of one of the large houses spilling cascades of blossom into Lantern Place. In the evenings the scent filled the air and often a blackbird perched on a branch to sing. It was there now shouting its heart out and the clear, determined notes vibrated in the still air. The scent of the lilac and the blackbird's song filled Iris with an indescribable longing: she felt that if only she could give vent in some way—sing, dance, or even run swiftly along some deserted shore—she would feel better.

Someone was coming through the alley. Not one of the family, she knew the sound of their feet. Not Maurice, she knew his, too. She stood by the gate holding her breath. This was Johnny's walk. She closed her eyes for fear she was mistaken because she knew that if she were wrong the disappointment would be almost unbearable. Next moment he was there and his hands were on her shoulders.

"Waiting for me at the gate. That's what I like to see," he said.

At first she almost believed she was dreaming but when he kissed her she could not doubt she was awake. Yet she was bewildered by his sudden appearance.

"I see the papers in Paris," he said. "I know what's been going on in the Yard, so I've taken leave to see what I can do to help. I'm thinking of giving up the bank."

"Oh, but you mustn't!" she protested. "It's safe and sure—at least it's bread and butter till you get a break with your songs."

"But we both said we'd help Ma if she ever needed us," he reminded her.

"Oh, Johnny, darling Johnny, I never meant you to do anything like this!" she cried. "Let's go in and see Auntie Camille —see what she has to say about it."

Aunt Camille and Ascot were delighted to see Johnny, but they were not so surprised at his suggestion as Iris had been because it was just the kind of thing his grandfather would have done, they said.

"You mustn't think of it, though," Aunt Camille said gravely. "I'm sure Melia won't hear of it."

"But I'm strong and hefty. Iris has always told me Ma needs a reliable man on the job and I'm the man," he said. "I've been wondering if we couldn't have a shop. We're all in this together, after all."

"But what happens when Tom comes home?" asked Ascot. "You've got to think how many can live out of a business—and families grow, you know," she added with a wink.

"At least I can make the offer," he said, "and in any case there's something else I want to see Ma about."

"What's that?" asked Iris.

"I want to ask her if I can marry you," he said. "Things are different now and I want to know if we can begin to think about it in earnest."

All of a sudden their marriage was not only possible, but probable. Before they had just been in love and their romance had been forbidden by the dictates of his father. Now his power was broken and their marriage was no longer something that lay in a far off future.

Iris looked round Aunt Camille's sitting room in which she had spent so many happy hours as she realized this and she felt a sudden, unfamiliar nostalgia. She loved Johnny with all her heart but when they were married she would still feel the pull of Lantern Place, she would still yearn to help Ma, she would still feel the claustrophobia for Tom. It was inescapable.

Ascot and Aunt Camille were watching her as she looked from one to the other and she knew they had divined her feelings. Then she looked at Johnny.

"You do want to marry me, don't you, Iris?" he asked.

"Yes," she said. "I love you very much."

20

MEANWHILE Melia was hurrying along the High Road towards Florrie's place. As she went she tried to think what the woman could possibly want with her and she hoped she was not on a fool's errand. Somehow she could not believe that Raymond would lead her on one. He seemed to be a good boy and she found herself wondering why, for his home life must have been as disrupted as Tom's.

Florrie had a small cottage beside the shed in which her mother had skinned rabbits in days gone by and Melia noticed that the whole place looked ramshackle and had none of the jauntiness of Florrie Perks herself. The coffee stall, once so clean and smart, was shut up and neglected.

Raymond answered her knock and took her straight into the front room. The light was poor but there was no disguising the squalor and untidiness there. The table was jumbled with crockery and pill boxes, the chairs were strewn with clothes, and some dreary looking socks hung on a line stretched across the small bay window. There was a television set in one corner and a large, tumbled bed took up the best part of a wall.

In this Melia saw Florrie Perks propped up against the pillows and she was horrified to see how haggard and ill she looked. Wrapped round her shoulders was the jacket of the jersey suit she had worn when she made her last, disastrous onslaught on the Yard.

"Well, Melia," she said, "I reckon you never expected to see me like this. Surprised you came, really."

"I could see the boy was worried," Melia replied. "Can't say it gives me any pleasure to see you looking so poorly."

"No. Well, I never done you much good and I can't last out much longer. Raymond don't like to hear me say that, but it's true just the same. They don't fool me with their cheerful talk, and feeling the way I do the sooner I quit the better."

"They'll get you right in hospital, Mum," said Raymond.

"They won't, duck, but you go on thinking so if it does you any good," said Florrie. "Go on now, go outside. I want to have a word with Melia in private."

After he had closed the door Florrie grinned suddenly and a shade of the old, wicked Perks audacity flitted across her face.

"It don't half seem funny to see you here, Melia," she said. "Listen, though. I want you to do something for me."

"What?" asked Melia cautiously.

"I know I didn't ought to have pinched Quick off of you, but I couldn't help myself. Maybe if I'd married him you'd have pinched him off me. No regrets. I got my two kids and I wouldn't have missed 'em for the world. I thought a lot of Quick, Melia. I guess I must have loved him. That's why I'm asking you if you'll take this place over."

"Take it over?" echoed Melia. "Whatever for?"

"Turn it into another Sparrow's Yard," said Florrie. "Come on, now. It's no good kidding yourself. Sparrow's Yard is finished but there's room here for another if the place is cleared up a bit. How about it?"

She leaned forward eagerly and a burning red patch appeared on each of her cheeks.

"You mean you want us all to come, the Tilleys and everyone?" asked Melia.

"That's right."

"But what about your own kids?"

"Selina's married, but Raymond's here, of course. I wondered if he could go in with you. Drive your van when you get one. You won't buy another horse if you've any sense."

"Well, I don't know I'm sure," said Melia. "Is Raymond willing?"

"You don't have to worry about him. He wants anything I want. He's easy to get on with—doesn't take after the Perks, you know."

"You're sure it's not just because you're feeling bad? How about when you get better?"

"I shan't get better," Florrie said. "But I'd feel a lot easier in my mind if you'd agree. You might say I'm doing it for Quick, or you might say I'm doing it because we're all in this together even though we've spent our lives fighting one another. When it boils down to it it's us, Melia, you and me and old square-faced Tilley against the Redmaynes, isn't it?"

"If you put it that way," Melia agreed.

"Then you'll come?"

"Right," said Melia. "I'll come, and I think the others will join me."

"Start when you like then. They're carting me off to the hospital tonight, so this is goodbye, Melia. Don't come and see me and for Gawd's sake don't let anyone send me flowers. Keep an eye on Raymond, that's all I ask."

"I'll do that," Melia promised.

She paused, wishing she could think of something else to say but nothing came. At least they understood each other.

"Goodbye, then, Florrie," she said.

Outside in the passage she laid her hand on Raymond's shoulder for a moment and said: "It's all right, Raymond. We'll do what your mum asks."

Raymond gulped. "Thanks," he said.

She opened the door and let herself out and as she closed it she heard an uncontrollable sob break from the boy. She did not like to go back and yet it seemed terrible to leave him there alone. She wished she had not heard that sob. She could imagine him trying to smother it, trying to control his feelings, and then relaxing for that fatal moment and giving way to his searing grief. Probably he was fighting to pull himself together now so that he could go back into that room and face his mother. She wondered if they would avoid each other's eyes or if they would talk of the future and speculate about it.

She squared her shoulders and started to plod along the High Road. My, but she was tired. By rights she ought to go straight home and tell the family what had happened but she wanted to think a bit first. Get the weight off her feet and sort her ideas out. Best thing would be a good glass of stout.

She went into the pub, bought her half pint and sat down. This move of Florrie's certainly put a different complexion on things and as she gazed round the familiar bar with its horse brasses, its china dishes and its prints of Villa Park, it seemed to look brighter, gayer, and altogether more alive. She knew, of course, that it had not altered one scrap since the last time she had been there and that the change was in herself.

No wonder. She was not under Cyril Redmayne's domination any more and now that she was free she was beginning to ask herself why she had not defied him when he blackmailed her into keeping Iris and Johnny apart. She had always told herself that her aim was to preserve their place in the Yard so that Tom would have something to come back to and she had even been ready to sacrifice her own daughter's happiness for that. No, not quite. She *had* been considering the other stallholders as well and yet had she been completely true to herself? The moment they heard his terms the others had made up their minds to leave the Yard as soon as they could. Even Mrs. Tilley, with Ernie on her hands, had not hesitated.

The fact was that she was frightened of anything new. That's what it was. She had clung to what she had always known as a child clings to its mother's skirts. Tom! Ten to one he would want to branch out on his own anyway and there would be the challenge of Raymond Perks to stimulate him now. They'd have to see how it all worked out, but in future she would steer clear of running other people's lives and she would not be afraid any more.

Suddenly she realized she was not alone. Mrs. Tilley had lumbered in with Alfie, and Winnie and Glad Cheek were up at the bar getting the drinks. They all came over and joined her.

"Look who's here," they said, just as though they were the chorus in a play.

"I think we've got something to celebrate tonight," Melia said, and she told them of Florrie's conciliatory gesture.

At first they could scarcely believe her, but gradually they took the news in and became more and more elated. Alfie went home to fetch his father and Winnie Cheek was dispatched to fetch Princess Potter.

"She wouldn't say nothing, but Princess don't like it outside the bank," Mrs. Tilley confided. "Very draughty, she says it is, and she feels sort of on show, not like when she was tucked away so nicely in the Yard. Ah well, we'll see what we can make of Florrie's place."

All the same, their delight and relief were tinged with a certain sorrow. Florrie had been a raucous, obstreperous, outrageous woman but she had always put them on their mettle and roused their fighting spirit. They hated to think of her ill and dying. As Mrs. Tilley remarked sombrely it was good news but it made the beer taste flat.

But by the time they parted that evening the stallholders of Sparrow's Yard had made their plans and decided to depart to their new quarters with dignity. They meant to go quietly and at once.

21

CYRIL REDMAYNE had been feeling uneasy for a long time and at the back of his mind was the constant fear that someone might expose the terms of his bargain with Melia Crockett. If the Press got hold of the story he shuddered to think what they would make of it. He wished he could retract the condition and if he could have seen Melia in the Yard he would have spoken to her about it. He could say he had been over-hasty, over-anxious, and he could appeal to her good sense as a parent. She would not be too stupid to see that a match between her daughter and his son was unsuitable. Perhaps, too, he ought to give that old man Wally Tagg something to compensate him for the loss of the stable.

Things had been going badly since they had come back to live at Villa Park and he had had such high hopes! Now the breach between himself and Helen was growing deeper and wider every day and with

Johnny away the house was silent and empty. Sometimes he caught himself listening for the piano.

About mid-day on Saturday he went down to see how the building was progressing. He did not relish the idea of making his way through the Yard with the inimical eyes of the stallholders on him. They always watched him now and he often saw them nudge a customer and mutter something which he guessed was uncomplimentary.

But when he reached the Yard it was empty—deserted. There was not a stall in sight, not a box or a crate or even so much as an odd stick of celery to betray the fact that there had ever been a market there.

He sat at the wheel of his car staring, unable to take in what he saw. This was what he had always wanted. All his life he had wanted to see the Yard clear, swept clean, free of the contamination of the barrow people. This was how his mother had wanted it and it had taken all these years to bring it about, but the sight of it now made him feel completely and utterly beaten.

With a sudden sense of awakening he